Ocean Pals:

Who Rescued Who?

Book 1

Jamie Mitchell Hadzick

This is a work of fiction. All of the character, organizations, places, animals and events portrayed in this novel are either products of the author's imagination or are used fictitiously. Any resemblance to actual persons, living or dead, business establishments, events, or locales is entirely coincidental.

To all the volunteers who work tirelessly to save
animals every day.

Chapter 1
CALEB and Camille

Her little boy wasn't so little anymore. Now that he was 12, he needed her less and less every day.

Damien was running across the wobbly bridge at the local Ocean Park playground playing tag with a few other kids from his school after their soccer practice. They were a little old to be playing on the equipment, however, they were respecting the younger kids' space and were blowing off some much needed steam.

Camille looked on, with a smile set across her pretty face and a little sorrow in her heart. Damien was her whole world and if he needed her less, what did that mean for her? Should she go back to work full-time?

She had a small law firm she ran from her home, but when Damien was born she cut her hours back to part-time to focus on him. Not wanting to lose herself completely, the 20-or-so hours she worked kept her sane, in the game, and contributing financially to their family.

Her husband, Max DiAngelo, made a good living as the local high school principal, but Camille wasn't ready to let go of her hard-earned career so quickly.

Catching herself lost in thought, she scanned the playground and park for Damien, unable to find him. He was tall for his age, so she could usually spot him pretty easily and his mocha skin stood out from the mostly alabaster tones at the park.

Dread started to drip into her bones when she still didn't see him over by the swings, practice fields, or parking lot and she rushed over to the other side to look for him. Rounding the large playset, her heart raced and goosebumps sprouted on her arms in fear—she was on the verge of panic.

Damien!

Damien!

Ducking through the swing set, dodging kids left and right, she used her whole body to look for him. Hands grabbed at poles, knees bent to look into the slides, arms helped her balance when she almost ran into a stroller, and sweat dripped down her back as her heart rate grew and grew.

Jolted back a step by a red splash of color over by the gazebo, Camille arched her body back to see over a crowd of teenagers gathered by the picnic tables. Relief engulfed her body as she tipped her head back and sighed.

There was Damien, in his red t-shirt, over by the old gazebo that was desperate for a coat of paint, about 200 yards from the playground. Annoyed at him for daring to leave without her permission, she walked over to see what he was doing.

Ready to give him a piece of her mind, her marching slowed as she saw why he was crouched down on the ground. About 20 feet past him was a black and white dog that nervously sniffed in the direction of her son and eyed him wearily.

"Damien," she whispered, "What are you doing? Whose dog is that?"

"Mom, hey, stay back. I'm trying to get him to come to me, so I can see if he has any tags on his collar."

"Baby, he might not be friendly. He looks scared. Let me take your place."

Recalling a post she saw on Facebook about not chasing after a loose dog and letting it come to you, she realized Damien had the right plan of action, but she didn't want him in harm's way.

"No, Mom, no. I got this. He already let me get this close. Do we have any food in the car?"

Not surprised by his go-getter attitude, but a bit taken back by his tone when he said "no," gave her pause to remember her earlier thoughts about him not needing her as much anymore.

"Yeah, we have some leftover fries. I'll be right back."

Jogging to her silver SUV, she used the key fob to unlock the doors and grabbed the take-out bag they had picked up earlier. While she ran back, she fished around the bag for something tasty to eat to entice the lost dog.

"Here," she said, handing an unwrapped burger to Damien, "This was for your dad."

He looked back to grab the sandwich and gave her a sly smile that made them both chuckle. His dad, Max, loved burgers and would be a little miffed that his Wednesday night cheat meal was going to a random dog.

Damien pulled the patty from between the bread, tore off a piece of meat, and threw it towards the stray. As the piece of burger came towards him, the dog squeezed his eyes shut and cowered his head lower as if bracing for impact. The burger landed right on his forehead and bounced off like it hit a trampoline. Landing in front of his paws, the smell must have wafted up and hit his nostrils, because his eyes popped open and he scurried around to locate the piece of former flying meat.

The dog gobbled down the bite of burger and looked to Damien with hopeful, but untrusting eyes.

"Come on, boy. I have more. It's okay, come here," Damien spoke quietly to the dog. "We won't hurt you, buddy. It's okay."

The dog moved a few feet closer while he sniffed the air and looked pensive. Damien threw him another piece of meat that landed a foot in front of his position.

The kid had pretty good aim.

The dog moved closer to find the treat and hungrily ate it up. This dance between a scared stray, and confident pre-teen dog whisperer, went on until the dog was only three or four feet away and Damien had one bite of burger left.

Moving his body so his shoulders faced away from the dog, Damien slowly reached out his hand, stretching his arms to their limit, to try and show the dog the last piece of meat.

"Buddy, this is all I have left. Can you come closer? I can't see if you have any tags on your collar."

Camille watched her son in awe. Where did he learn how to handle a situation like this? Who taught him this stuff and, more importantly, what in the hell were they going to do once they had the pup?

The dog inched toward Damien and Damien inched toward the dog.

Both moved at the speed of molasses. They seemed to have a silent understanding between them that if one moved too fast, the other was outta there.

As the dog gently stretched for the last bite of burger, Damien slipped the treat into his mouth and, carefully, reached a little farther to scratch behind his ear. The dog froze for a few seconds. He looked confused and unsure, but let the scratching continue. He leaned in a little more, slowly closed his eyes, and let out a long sigh that spoke volumes about how little love he had received lately.

Camille noted how the muscular dog looked worn and tired, like he'd been out on his own for a while. He had long toenails that looked almost painful, astonishingly protruding ribs, and dirty fur that wore many scratches and scars from old wounds. This poor dog had been lost and fending on his own for god knows how long.

While he had the dog under his ear-scratching spell, Damien took off his belt, slipped an end through the dog's nylon collar, and fed it back through the buckle to create a makeshift leash. Once the dog was secured, it was like a light bulb went off and he realized he was safe and that someone was being nice to him, maybe for the first time ever. His tail wagged so hard it wiggled his entire body and he started to cover Damien in overly appreciative kisses.

"Wow, great idea, Damien. Did you see someone do that on TV or something?"

"No, Mom," he scoffed at her, "I saw it on YouTube. I follow a dog rescue and they posted a video about what to do if you find a lost dog."

Again, there was that tone that reminded her of her dwindling role in his life.

"Can we keep him?"

"No, we can't keep him. Duke might not like having another dog in the house. He likes that he's king of the castle."

Damien looked forlorn.

"Well, we can't take him to the county shelter. They put dogs down! I can't let that happen. Look how bad he looks. He needs a family!"

Damien nearly shook with emotion. It was clear this event, and this dog, meant a lot to him and he wasn't about to let his new friend have a bad ending.

"We can look for a different shelter. A safer one," Camille said, while wondering how Damien knew about euthanasia and animal shelters.

"A no-kill one," Damien confidently remarked, "They don't put a time limit on how long a dog can stay. I heard about it online."

More YouTube education, Camille guessed.

"Alright, we'll look one up and see what we can find. Let's get to the car. It's starting to get dark. And hey, next time you decide to wander off, please let me know. I was starting to worry."

"I know. Sorry, Mom," Damien mumbled as they made their way to the car.

There was that pre-teen attitude rearing its ugly head again.

Chapter 2

KONA and Sammi

The locker room door slammed open and laughter bounced off the walls as the young girls filed in before practice. Steel or aluminum, who knew which, clanged together over and over again as the girls opened and closed their assigned lockers to grab their grips and remove their shoes and street clothes.

Leotards, or leos as everyone called them, were their attire for every practice and most of the girls had 10 or more in their collections. Chattering away about their days while they smoothed out their ponytails, added biker shorts over their leos, and tape to their wrists or ankles, none of the girls noticed that the one bathroom stall never went unoccupied during their stay in the locker room.

After they emptied out to the main gym for practice, Sammi dragged herself from the stall and went over to the small mirror and sink to wash her hands and clean up her face. Black eyeliner was smudged under her blue eyes that were red rimmed from tears. Angrily wiping it away, she let out a long sigh and internally berated herself for letting him get to her again.

Him.

Her ex-boyfriend.

He left her high and dry seven months ago after being together for ten years.

She knew they were having problems, but he didn't want to try anymore. He didn't want to work on it and ended things one night without much emotion or empathy. She knew now that he had checked out of their relationship months before, which was why he was able to bounce back and move on so quickly and easily.

That's why she was crying in the bathroom at the gymnastics center, Ocean Tumblers, where she worked. Thanks to freakin' Facebook, she found out he had a new girlfriend and from all his recent posts, it seemed like he was infatuated with her . . . even though she appeared to be everything he once said he hated.

Glancing at her watch, knowing she was late to warm ups, Sammi clapped her hands over her cheeks a few times to snap herself back into reality and whispered a quick, "Come on, freaking pull yourself together!"

After coaching the competitive girls team all evening, Sammi pulled up to her mother's house a little after 9:30pm, exhausted and ready for a shower, her jammies, and bed. The brick tri-level home held many wonderful memories from her childhood, but being back here now, felt like she had failed.

She didn't have anywhere to go after the breakup and found herself standing on her mom's doorstep, asking if she could stay for a while. Of course, her mom said yes and ushered her inside for a cup of tea, a shot of whiskey, and a shoulder to cry on.

Sammi wanted to save for a house of her own, and renting an apartment put a wrench in that plan, so that's why she was back with good old mom. Oh, and because she relied too much on that douchebag of an ex-boyfriend.

Once inside, she realized her mom was already in bed, but she had left Sammi a note on the two-person dining table in the kitchen that read—

"Hope you had a great day, honey! I'm going to the shelter tomorrow afternoon. Want to come with? Love you!"

To help keep her busy during retirement, her mom, Ruth, volunteered at a no-kill animal shelter twice a week. She loved the animals and was always encouraging Sammi to tag along, explaining that it might make her feel better and help her meet some new people.

Since the breakup, Sammi had been low on money, confidence, and friends. Her entire life had been entwined with Mark and untangling it all left her vulnerable and amazed at how reliant she had become on a man.

The next morning, she woke up to her mom's loud swearing coming from downstairs.

"Shit! Sammi! Shit! Shit! Sammi!" bellowed Ruth from the hard tile floor in the foyer.

Rushing down to see what was going on, Sammi found her mom in a heap, grabbing at her side.

"I think I broke my fucking hip!" she yelled.

Instantly awake, Sammi threw on some clothes, grabbed their toothbrushes, and gingerly scooped her mom up and maneuvered her into the car. Once at the orthopedic hospital, after some x-rays, they learned that Ruth did, in fact, break her fucking hip.

"Surgery?" cried Ruth, "Oh my god, I cannot believe this. Old people break their hips. I'm not that old, am I?" She asked anxiously.

She gazed at Sammi, who swore up and down that, no, she wasn't old and no, she couldn't believe it either.

That's when Ruth realized she'd be unable to help at the shelter for the next few weeks.

"Sammi, you have to go in for me. My babies need you there. The shelter is already so short on volunteers and I was going to start picking up a third shift each week to help." She rubbed her temples with her fingers and groaned, "This isn't happening."

"Mom, I don't know anyone there and haven't done the volunteer training yet."

"I already texted Emily and told her you were coming before I slipped down those damn stairs. She texted back that it was no problem and that she'd be happy to go over the shelter rules and procedures with you today. I'm sure she still will. Here, hand me my phone. I'll call her now," Ruth demanded with a sharp point of her finger.

It didn't seem like there was any reason to fight her on this since she was already dialing, so Sammi just let it happen.

Off to the shelter I go, she thought. *Hopefully, it's better than this stuffy hospital room.*

Sammi pulled her red Scion up to the bright blue building and into a parking spot. The single-story, block building looked like an old house that was converted into an animal shelter. Locking up behind her, she walked toward the entrance and noticed little paw prints painted all over the sidewalks leading her inside. A cute, little touch to brighten up an otherwise drab walkway.

She pulled open the heavy door and looked around the lobby. It smelled like every other animal shelter, pet store, or vet's office she'd ever been in. To the left was a cabinet full of shirts for sale along with a door leading to the dog run area. To the right was a large reception desk, a birdcage with a parrot inside, a row of doors that led to three, small offices, and a cat adoption room in the far back.

"Can I help you?" came a voice from behind the desk.

Sammi looked up to see a woman with short gray hair, kind eyes, knobby fingers, and a deep voice.

"Hi, I'm Sammi Banks. My mom is Ruth Banks, she's a volunteer here and—"

The lady cut her off and jumped in, "Oh yeah, she called me earlier. I'm Emily. How's she doing?"

"Good but pissed that she's down and out for a while."

Emily chuckled, "Yeah, she gave me an ear full about it on the phone. I sympathize with her though. It sucks getting older."

They both shrugged and stood in awkward silence for a few beats before Emily jumped back in, "Well, it's awfully nice of you to sub in for her while she's recovering. Let me show you around and get you to sign some forms."

Sub in?

Sammi's mind was focused on this statement while Emily pulled some paperwork from behind the counter and added it to a clipboard.

Do they think I'm covering all of her shifts?

Reeling from the day's events, her mouth wouldn't open to question Emily. She just followed her instructions by filling out the paperwork and tried to listen as she took her through the shelter for a tour.

After going over all the procedures and shelter rules, they headed to the outdoor dog area. The dogs had inside and outside access through doggie doors in the wall, but they were always fully secured in their own run by six-foot fencing. To access the dogs, there were doors on either side and the interior ones were Dutch doors, which allowed you to open just the top half or just the bottom half. The run area was small, but well maintained with easy-to-clean turf grass and six-foot vinyl fencing. There was a concrete bench sitting against the side of the building to rest tired feet, an old, plastic milk crate secured to the wall about four feet from the ground that held a variety of tennis balls, and a small shelf to set drinks, poop bags or phones.

As soon as she spotted Sammi and Emily, she came bounding towards them with friendly eyes and an adorable grin. She was about as wide as a mac truck but was the most beautiful brindle color. Sammi reached her hand out to let the dog sniff her but instead, the happy girl went right in for a kiss.

Sammi's worries about the subbing in for her mom started to fade away. She lowered to her haunches to get more kisses and to find a better angle for optimum ear scratching.

"Her name is Kona. She was adopted out from Ocean Pals a year ago but was returned yesterday because they didn't want her anymore," Emily said, her annoyance at the former adopters' obvious. "They never walked her, basically ignored her, got her fat, and then dumped her back here without a second thought. Freakin' people."

Hearing Kona's story resonated with Sammi and melted away any worry she had left about volunteering. She decided right then and there that she'd be happy to fill in a few times a week and meet more of these grateful creatures.

She too had been taken in by a stranger, treated poorly, basically ignored, fattened up, and dumped without much care recently.

They were two peas in a sad little pod.

Chapter 3

CHARLOTTE and Willa

As she pulled from her driveway to the main road, Willa Atkins thought about the past four years of her life. She had gotten divorced, sent two kids off to college, started volunteering more regularly, and lived alone for the first time in almost three decades. A lot had changed and while some of it was sad, like her kids leaving for college, she was proud of her volunteer efforts and her ability to move on from her ex-husband and thrive without him.

Their marriage had never been picture perfect but it wasn't until 10 or so years ago when his eyes started to wander. She forgave him the first time, even though she was gutted at his infidelity, and he swore up and down that it would never happen again.

Liar, liar, pants on fire.

Willa wasn't sure how many more affairs Thomas had but she knew of at least three. She always thought she would have packed her bags and been outta there at the first sign of another fling but, surprisingly, she just chose to ignore it. It was the easiest way for her to deal with it—to just push it out of her mind.

All of that ignoring came to a crashing halt when her son, Dalton, saw Thomas out with one of his side chicks and confronted them about it publicly and very loudly. Hearing about the confrontation secondhand didn't soften the blow for Willa.

Rumor had it Dalton took no mercy while verbally berating his father for cheating on his mother and it all went down at Thomas's most high-end restaurant, Waves, which was always packed. He owned a slew of restaurants in Ocean Park, which he hoped to hand down to his kids someday.

Dalton came home furious and ready to console Willa. He thought she was in the dark about the affair and was ready to break the news to her, believing it was for the best. When he found out Willa already knew about the affairs, his anger turned towards her. He found it unbelievable that she would stay with Thomas, knowing he snuck around, and was unrelenting in his stance that she should have left him years ago.

Things between them improved but Willa knew Dalton was still sore with her over the whole thing, even years later. Her daughter, Dede, wasn't nearly as upset and took the whole ordeal in stride. She'd always been that way—very understanding, slow to judge, and quick to forgive.

Thomas and Willa divorced as amicably as you could when one person cheated for 10 years. In the split, Willa got their rental home on the bay and a portion of Thomas's restaurant profits. They split custody of the kids, but it was mostly a moot point since Dalton was almost 18 at the time and Dede 14.

Thomas kept their family home, although he went on to sell it almost immediately after the split, stating he needed a fresh start. Willa believed he needed the money now that her trust fund was out of the picture, but she didn't mind that he sold the house, because she got what she wanted—the bay home.

The house sat on the water in a quiet community of bay front properties. They paid double what the homes on the other side of the inlet sold for because their community was spread out and the houses weren't right on top of each other. The Atkins didn't want to be packed in like sardines and Willa was so glad they made the splurge then, rather than waiting until now, as home prices have jumped astronomically.

The house was a beach cottage on stilts that had three bedrooms, two bathrooms, an open floor plan, and a large wrap around deck. The lot was spacious but mostly covered in pine trees, which helped keep the lawn maintenance down and they had 200 feet of water frontage. There was a small wooden dock where Willa could put her kayak into the water or where she could sit to watch the sun disappear into the evening with a glass of wine.

All those thoughts kept her mind occupied so when she pulled up to the shelter, she was a little surprised that she didn't remember her drive over. She parked, locked up her Lexus SUV, and headed inside, where she saw a woman she didn't recognize talking to Emily. She said a quick hello to Quincy, the resident parrot, who squawked, "hello" back to her, a gesture he only saved for those who knew him best.

Willa was comfortable here at Ocean Pals Animal Shelter. She had been volunteering for the last eight years and knew the people and animals like the back of her hand. Since she was such a seasoned volunteer, she was asked to take on more responsibilities than most. She helped with normal tasks, like cleaning up cages, doing laundry, walking dogs, socializing the cats, and greeting visitors, but she also was asked to take photos of the animals, run volunteer orientations, plan special events, and manage the volunteer Facebook group and text chain. The shelter was low on volunteers, so they needed someone like Willa to keep morale high, engage volunteers who missed their shifts, and encourage everyone to spread the word about the shelter's efforts.

First things first though, she had to greet the dogs. Opening the door to the long corridor immediately instructed the dogs to begin their chorus of barks, howls, yips, and yaps. They sang to her as she went from kennel to kennel, or condos as she liked to call them to make it sound less sterile, and she greeted them with love and admiration. Reaching the end of the row, on the left-hand side, was her girl, Charlotte.

"Hey, Char, how are we doing today?" she asked the hound mix who replied back to her with her signature bay,

"Ahrooo!"

"We'll go on a walk later, my girl, but I need to get some stuff done first."

"Roooo roo!" Charlotte complained.

"I promise!"

Charlotte was the shelter's longest resident. She had been transferred to Ocean Pals two years ago from a different shelter that was in a rural area. Ocean Pals would often help take the burden off those rural or overcrowded shelters when they had the extra space. Most dogs came in, spent a few weeks in the shelter, and then found their forever home. The shelter held a lot of events and aggressively marketed the dogs to get them adopted, but no one ever came for Charlotte.

She was a bit of a difficult egg. She needed to be the only dog in a home, she pulled like a hellion on the leash, she could be loud due to her vocal hound dog nature, and she was pushing six years old. None of those things mattered to some people, but most were looking for a dog that would be a little less work and a little younger than Charlotte.

That's why Charlotte was Willa's favorite. She had sass and something to say and wasn't going to change it for the wrong person. She was older and misunderstood, a lot like Willa. People counted her out and most never expected her to get adopted by a normal family. They figured a volunteer would feel so bad for her that they'd end up taking her home out of pity. Charlotte would sense that and she'd hate it. She wanted her own person and was willing to wait for them.

Willa slipped Charlotte a treat and headed to the outside dog area where the new woman and Emily were sitting with Kona.

The 30-something woman was hunkered down petting Kona with furrowed brows and a tight look on her face. Willa heard Emily explaining why Kona was returned and how they had her on a strict diet to help her slim down and become more comfortable and healthy.

"Hey, ladies. Hi, Kona. How are we doing today?" Willa asked when she walked up.

"Hey there, Willa. This is Sammi. She's a new volunteer," Emily said. "Her mom is Ruth Banks."

Willa reached out a hand as Sammi stood up to greet her and they shook.

"I'm Sammi, nice to meet you. What was your name again?" she questioned curiously.

"It's Willa," she chuckled, "My mom was a big hippie and wanted to call me Wildflower but, thankfully, my dad talked her into Willa instead. I see you've met Kona. She's a sweetheart, isn't she?"

"Oh my god, she's the best. I can't believe her old owners," Sammi said with a shake of her head and frown on her face.

"Well, if you stick around here long enough, you'll learn that people are the absolute worst."

Willa was doing some laundry when Zak, the shelter's most dependable employee, knocked on the doorframe to grab her attention.

"Hey, can you help me with an intake real quick? The lady has some questions and I need to get the dog vetted and ready before I leave in an hour."

"Sure, lead the way."

Zak led Willa out from the small room that was both laundry, cleaning, and storage to the lobby where a petite woman and her son were standing holding a pitbull on what looked to be a makeshift leash.

"This is one of our long-term volunteers, Willa." Zak said, "And Willa, this is Camille. She and her son found this dog running loose at Ocean Park Playground earlier today."

The two women shook hands and smiled, while the boy nudged at his mom.

"I'm Camille and this is Damien," she said as she nodded towards her pre-teen son. "I'd be lying if I said I found the dog. Damien found him and spent 40 minutes coaxing him over to us with a fast-food burger. It was pretty inspiring to watch, although I wish he'd have that much patience with his homework," she said with a wink.

"Moooom," Damien groaned with an embarrassed eye roll that might have reached the back of his brain.

Willa chuckled at the two, remembering how it was with her kids when they were Damien's age and how anything and everything could embarrass them.

"Zak said you have a few questions. What can I help you with?"

"We just want to make sure this guy gets the help he deserves. You're a no-kill shelter, right? He won't be put down if he doesn't get adopted? We can't keep him because we have a dog at home who isn't fond of other dogs getting all his attention."

Camille emphasized "his" with raised eyebrows that indicated their dog at home was spoiled rotten and knew it too.

"That's right. He'll be safe here until he finds his forever home."

"Great, right, Damien?"

The boy gave a small nod, but his shoulders had rolled forward, his eyes downcast, and his fingers that softly rubbed the dog's ears made it obvious he wasn't ready to let him go.

Camille glanced back to Willa, gave her a small smile, and whispered, "This is our first time finding a stray and I don't think it'll be his last. He's a huge dog lover and I think leaving them here is going to be the hardest part for him."

Willa nodded her understanding. She'd found many stray dogs and cats in her lifetime, or maybe they found her, but either way, the bond you formed with an animal you saved was instantaneous and as strong as steel.

"How do you guys pay for all of this?" Camille asked while she looked around the large lobby.

"Mostly private donations but we put on a lot of events and fundraise all year long. Plus, the building was donated through an estate and most of the people you see helping out are volunteers. There are only a few employees."

"Volunteers, huh? How does that work?"

"Anyone over the age of 16 can volunteer and we ask that everyone pick a three-hour shift once a week. We have a variety of tasks that need done so you can float around as needed. Kids 12 to 15 can volunteer at our events, but they need to be accompanied by a parent or guardian and we don't typically let them help out directly with the animals due to liability."

As she nodded in agreement, Camille looked impressed and possibly interested. Since the shelter was low on volunteers, Willa decided to take a shot. What did she have to lose?

"Would you be interested in volunteering? We're always looking for extra help," she said with a smile. "We're just about to have a volunteer meeting if you'd like to pop in and join us. Damien can come too, or we can let him hang out with this guy a little longer," she said motioning to the stray dog.

Without missing a beat, Camille smiled and agreed to stay for the meeting.

"Why not?"

Chapter 4

HOMER and JC

"Sorry, I'm late! My meeting with my caterer went long!" JC exclaimed as he ran into the room with his arms full of papers, binders, and a half-full coffee drink from Starbucks.

Everyone watched as he set down his coffee and stuffed binders, huffed, and smoothed out his black hair.

"Your caterer is Ryan . . . your husband," Willa said with a laugh.

"I know you know that, but maybe everyone else didn't. Way to call me out Wil-la," he said with a head tilt and shoulder shrug.

Everyone laughed and JC glanced around the room.

"Packed house today, ladies. This is great. For all that don't know me, I'm JC Diaz and I'm hosting this month's volunteer meeting. Typically, either Emily, Willa, or I run these meetings and lucky for all you newbies, it's my turn this month," JC said with a little swing of his hips.

"Since we have some new faces here today, let's go around and introduce ourselves real quick. Y'all know me already, but I'll give a little more detail since I know you're all dying to know. I'll be 30 in three weeks—ugh, kill me now," he said with a grunt and drop of his head. "My husband is Ryan Diaz and he owns a catering company and food truck that makes its way around Berlin every week. If any of you wanted to try some amazing Asian-style vegan food, hit up his food truck. I swear the man is a genius with a grill."

"Anyways, we've been married for three years. I own and run a club in Ocean City proper called Spinners. I didn't name it so don't give me those judgy looks. I bought it five years ago when I retired from baseball and needed something new to do that resembled a career."

Everyone giggled and Camille chimed in with a sly grin, "Oh, so that's where you got those amazing arms from then, huh? Baseball." She emphasized her words with a few eyebrow wiggles at the end.

"Why, yes I did, and they are my husband's second favorite thing about me," he said with a devilish grin.

The room erupted in laughter, cheers, and squeals of appreciation. Once everyone calmed and JC's red cheeks returned to their normal tan, caramel, he continued.

"I'm originally from Puerto Rico, but my family moved here when I was a baby. I love these shelter animals because they don't care where you're from, what you look like, who you love, how you identify, or what political party you follow. If you love them, they'll love you back and I can't think there's anything better in the world than that."

Sobered by his truth talk and how poignant his statements, everyone nodded in appreciation but kept quiet.

"Okay, now that I gave you my full biography. It's your turn. Start us off Willa."

"Yeah, well, mine will be much quicker. I'm Willa and I have two children who're in college. I've been a volunteer for eight years and I love everything about these special animals. If you want to know more about me, you'll have to get to know me. I don't give it up as easily as JC does," she said with a smirk.

To her left was Sammi, who jumped in next.

"I'm Sammi Banks. This is my first day here, but my mom volunteers a few times a week now that she's retired. She broke her hip today so I'm filling in for her while she recovers. I'm a gymnastics coach in the evenings at Ocean Tumblers, so I'll be looking for daytime volunteer shifts, if possible."

Everyone's eyes moved to Emily as Sammi finished up.

"Hi, I'm Emily. I've been volunteering here for 20 years, so Ocean Pals feels a bit like home to me. I'm windowed but have three wonderful grown children who all live in the tri-state area. I foster for Ocean Pals and have Vito at home now. He's a three-year old rottweiler, boxer mix who will be coming back to the shelter in a few weeks to start his adoption journey. He needed some time to heal from wounds he sustained from being a bait dog for a dog fighting ring."

The new members of the group gasped at hearing this.

"He wouldn't fight, so they made him a bait dog, which is how they get the other dogs hyped up for their fights. The poor guy was saved when the whole operation was raided, but he has scars that go deeper than his superficial wounds. We'll get him a forever home though—don't you worry.

Since I've been here so long, don't be afraid to ask for my help."

Camille cleared her throat to begin, "Hi, I'm Camille DiAngelo. My son and I looked up no-kill shelters this afternoon because we, well, he found a stray dog and he didn't want him going to the county shelter. I'm interested in learning more about what you all do here and how I can help as a volunteer. I'm an attorney and run a small practice out of my home part-time. My husband is the principal at Cape Henlopen High School and we've been lucky to call Ocean Park our home for the last 13 years."

"Oh, girl, we'll be happy to have you here, as well as your expertise as a lawyer," JC said.

These round-the-room introductions continued until the whole group was covered and then JC jumped right into their monthly meeting agenda.

JC tried his best to stay focused and to listen to everyone's ideas, but his mind was elsewhere. It's true he had been at a meeting with his caterer husband, Ryan, but they weren't discussing food or an upcoming event. They were dissecting the club's books, trying to understand how its finances had gotten so off balance and out of hand. Ryan was worried that JC wasn't taking the financial folly seriously enough and demanded that he hire an accountant to get a better handle on things.

It wasn't that JC didn't think the lopsided balance sheet was a big deal, but he believed he could turn it around by holding a few extra special events at the club in the next few months. His shindigs always drew a crowd from far and wide and brought in money that he was desperate for.

Hiring a new accountant would cost money and JC wasn't one to trust quickly. Sure, he made friends wherever he went but he kept those people at arm's length. To them, he was always the happy, fun guy who was the life of the party, but that was only one part of him. He didn't let many people in to see the more sensitive, worrisome man hiding behind the smile.

He pulled himself from his thoughts just in time to end the meeting and he thanked everyone before he popped out to visit with his favorite dog. Homer was on the sick side of the shelter and wouldn't be available for adoption until he recovered from his heartworm treatment. He'd be okay in a month or so but had to be kept on limited activity, so he wouldn't get too excited and dislodge any worms currently being eradicated by the meds.

Homer was a big mastiff mix whose ears had been poorly cropped, leaving little stubs with no earflaps. He was most likely born by a backyard breeder who inhumanely cut at his ears, having no idea what he was doing, and maimed the dog in the process. Backyard breeders were in it for the quick cash and didn't give a damn about the dog's well-being, treatment, or what kind of home they ended up in.

Despite his horrific upbringing, Homer radiated sunshine with those he trusted. Wet, sloppy kisses, full body cuddles, and backbreaking wiggles were Homer's specialty when it came to his people. Although he was slow to trust, he came around faster than JC. Show him a few days of love, compassion, and butt scratches and you were in like Flynn with Homer.

His blue coat shined now that he was getting good food and proper care, so when JC rounded the corner to greet him, Homer glimmered even brighter than normal. He was engaged in a full-blown wiggle butt dance that almost had his tail hitting him on the sides of his head each time he wagged his whole body.

"Whoa boy, calm down! No need to freak out. I'm here to hang with you. It's good to see you too, buddy," JC said to Homer as he opened his kennel door and entered his condo. "I have a few minutes to cuddle if you're so inclined. Would you be up for that?"

Homer lapped big kisses over JC's face while he bent down to sit on the cold, concrete floor.

"I'll take that as a yes to cuddling," JC joked as Homer gave him no time to get comfortable before he plopped his 90-pound, muscular but heavy body into JC's lap.

Checking to make sure no one was around before he started to speak, JC rubbed Homer between the ears, which served to comfort them both.

"I've had quite a day, buddy. The club is in some serious trouble and I'm hoping I can find my way out of it. I'm only 60% sure I can and that dang 40% is making me nervous. Ryan's worrying isn't helping either. But I get it, you know? He wants us to save as much as we can now and not go dwindling down into a debt hole. I told you he wants to adopt next year, right?" JC spoke to the dog like he was going to answer back and to JC, he did. Homer's huffs, nudges of his nose, eye movements and eyebrow expressions gave away exactly what he was feeling.

Homer huffed and lightly licked his hand.

"Yeah, I know, next year is crazy to me though. I know he wants this and I know I want this, but I don't want to screw it up before we even get started with the whole process, you know? They're going to dig into our finances and our personal lives and if they find a broke club owner who can't manage his own business, they're going to drop us before we make it to the plate, you know?"

Homer whined and dropped his head to JC's knee with a grunt.

"Ex-nay on the baseball references, got it. I don't know why you hate those. They're a homerun with everyone else," JC egged him on.

Homer lifted his big, blocky head to look up at JC. His eyes were caramel colored with gold, glittery specks. His eyebrows, littered with gray hairs, rose ever so slightly and his wide mouth opened just a sliver to let out a tiny, chihuahua-sized bark that told JC just how unfunny he was at the moment.

"Okay, bud, I hear you. You're looking good and soon you'll be moved across the building, over to the well side, and will be available for adoption. You'll find your forever home. I know you will. I'm going to miss you so damn much, but I'll be so stoked for you."

JC squeezed Homer in a big hug and felt his soft fur on his face. Homer leaned into JC's body, removing any possible space between them and covered his hands and knees in kisses, since they were the only parts of him he could reach. They stayed there, cuddled, and spooning for another minute before JC broke the bad news to Homer.

"Alright, bud, I gotta go. I'm sorry for the short visit today, but you need your rest and I need a cocktail and an Accounting for Dummies book. Do you think YouTube will explain it better than a book?" he asked the dog as he stood.

Homer tilted his head to the side and looked up through his eyebrows, gutting JC with his perfect rendition of puppy eyes.

"Ugh, bud, you know I can't handle the puppy eyes," JC moaned.

Reaching out for one more kiss, Homer laid it on thick by lowering his giant head more, pulling his jowls down into an almost frown-like shape, and using his silky-colored eyes to pierce JC's soul.

"You're too damn good at that, bud. Use that on everyone who walks by your condo when you're on the well side and you're as good as adopted, you spoiled rotten little minx!"

Homer barked and licked JC's hand through the kennel door. It was their version of a high five. JC headed towards the door, with heartache for Homer and a stomachache from his bad business dealings.

Chapter 5

ATHENA and Sammi

It was a bad day.

Waking up was really what started Sammi's whole day on a downward trajectory. Her confidence was in the shitter and her motivation down the drain, right there with it. That aching, dull pit of sadness followed her everywhere and she was sick and tired of feeling so damn miserable. Breakups were hard but they weren't supposed to be this bad if they were with such a shithead, right?

That statement haunted her. She knew her ex wasn't the amazing, sexy beast that she was meant to be with, but she was struggling to kick her attachment to him, and maybe her reliance on him.

They'd been together for a long time and he was her friend, confidant, and supporter through many years. Sure, they sucked as a couple but that didn't mean there wasn't some love there. She relied on him too much though, for friendships, money, emotional support, and motivation. She needed to find those things for herself now.

Bad mood in tow, she yanked her car door open and rolled her eyes while she got in. She didn't want to do anything today, let alone volunteer at the shelter, where she'd do laundry, pick up poop, and deal with rowdy dogs. The only reason she was going in was because she had to get away from her mom. She was driving her crazy with all her requests while she recovered from her surgery. She loved her and all, but damn, she was a handful when she was bored.

Sammi finally arrived at the shelter and was pretty sure the rest of the town was happy that she was parked and off the roads. Her sour mood had surged her road rage driving and took her from a yellow alert level to a red on the disaster scale. She grabbed her bag and dragged her tired, stupid feet inside. She sure does act like a grown up, doesn't she?

She signed in and saw that no other volunteers were there yet.

Great, this should be fun.

Her mood was only worsened by the increased level of responsibility she'd have since she was the only volunteer there now. She usually stopped in to say hi to all the dogs before getting to work but today, their barking and carrying on was only going to make her head hurt.

Laundry seemed like a good place to start since it was piled up about four feet high and reeked of pee. She started a load and then pulled the blankets and towels from the dryer to fold and put them away. Most of the supplies were kept in this small laundry room. There were large shelves for all the dog beds, towels, and blankets and kitchen-like cabinets for the bowls, utensils, wet food, and cleaning supplies. Dog and cat toys were thrown into old kitty litter buckets under the utility sink, which sat next to a raised porcelain tub used for bath time.

While the laundry spun and dried, Sammi headed over to the two mountains of stainless-steel dog bowls that needed cleaned out, rinsed, dried, and put away. She started on this mind-numbing task and zoned out while scrub-a-dub-dubbing her way through the stacks. Still irritated, she felt her rage grow even more when she knocked a stack of 10 bowls onto the floor, which created a monumentous marching band sized percussion that they probably heard two streets over.

Her food bowl rendition of the classic cafeteria plate spill didn't bring any embarrassing applause like in middle school, but it did bring in a lady who was in the volunteer meeting with her the other day.

"Oh damn, you okay?" she asked while she bent down to help clean up the mess.

"Yeah, I'm fine, just a klutz moment. Sorry for all the noise."

"No problem." She chuckled, "I have a pre-teen son at home who is obsessed with his new drum kit, so I'm totally used to it. He is terrible," she drew out the ending with a sigh.

They both laughed before she introduced herself.

"I'm Camille, I was at the meeting here the other day. I'm just starting my volunteer journey, so feel free to tell me if I'm doing anything wrong or if I can jump in and help anywhere."

"Oh cool, I'm still new too but have done a handful of shifts. I'm Sammi."

After introductions were made and the bowls were cleaned up, the ladies headed out to the yard to start rotating the dogs out of their kennels.

"So, just make sure all the cages are locked first before you let anyone out. Sometimes they stick and don't click in the whole way, so if one of the bigger dogs jumps up on their door, they can push it open," Sammi said to Camille while she checked the first few doors were locked tight.

"Sounds good. I'll work on the other side."

After all the doors were secured, they left the first dog on the right side out of her cage. Her name was Athena and she was as pretty as her goddess-given name. Shiny, beige fur with long, lean legs, and a muscular build, she ran up and down the fake grass to stretch out her cramped muscles. Stopping to squat to pee, she looked up and showed them her yellow eyes that shined in the sunlight.

"Man, she is striking. Her eyes are just gorgeous," Camille said, taking the words right out of Sammi's mouth.

"Yeah, she's beautiful but a lot of people pass by her because she's a little aloof in her cage. They want a dog who's going to wag and get excited about people, but I think . . . I think she's just been here so long that she doesn't have the strength to act all excited, get her hopes up, and then be disappointed when they walk away and decide to meet a young lab puppy or a small shih tzu instead."

Sammi eyed Athena absentmindedly, "But, I get where she's coming from. It hurts to be let down over and over again."

Sammi realized Camille hadn't said anything in response, so she looked towards her and found her watching with her head tilted to the side and eyebrows pulled in.

"What's up," she asked nervously.

Drawing in a slow breath, she took a moment before she answered.

Her soft eyes rested on Sammi and with a gentle voice asked, "You're hurting, aren't you?"

The look on her face, the pure care that radiated from Camille's eyes burrowed through Sammi and struck in her core. Her stomach tied up in knots and her eyes burned as she held back tears, refusing to let her tattered life rule her emotions.

Sammi tried to swallow the tennis ball-sized lump in her throat and avoided eye contact at all costs before she answered, "Yeah, it's been a tough, few months. I guess the dogs and I have a little something in common."

"You're all looking for a fresh start," Camille said in a soft, gentle voice that immediately warmed Sammi's heart.

She nodded and choked back her emotions that threatened to boil over.

Camille's voice was easy and quiet, "I know we just met, but it looks like we're going to be volunteer buddies, so you can vent all you want to me and the dogs. We won't tell anyone."

A smile pulled at Sammi's lips and her awful mood seemed to release its stranglehold from her neck. She forced a small smile and felt a tick better than she did this morning. Maybe getting out of the house and volunteering here wasn't so bad.

"Thanks. I really appreciate that. And I'll take you up on it ... but don't say I didn't warn you," She said as she moved her hands in large circles in front of her body, "I've got a wholllle lot of crap going on."

They both laughed and Camille bent down to greet Athena, but continued to look at Sammi, her silence encouraged her to continue.

She obliged.

"A few months ago, my ex dumped me for another woman. We were together for 10 years."

Camille's face registered surprise, and then understanding, but she stayed quiet, so Sammi continued.

"And while the breakup part sucks, the worst part of the whole thing is that I let myself rely on him so much. My life was so wrapped up in his and I lost myself in the process. I had to move home to live with my mom because, among everything else, I relied on him financially too."

Camille continued to pet Athena and gently scratched at the back of her skull between her ears. The beautiful dog had her eyes closed and looked like she was in heaven. They were both quiet and let Sammi continue.

"It's not like I didn't work or contribute to the relationship, but I'm a gymnastics coach, so I didn't make as much as he did and he loved spending money and buying expensive things. He's a doctor and I felt I had to keep up with his lifestyle, so I never saved anything."

Camille spoke up, "You were together for 10 years? Did you have a joint bank account or anything? Did he know you struggled to match his more expensive lifestyle?"

"No, we were strangely independent in many ways. We didn't watch tv together most nights like a lot of people do. I'd watch my shows in the family room while he watched his shows in the living room. Same with dinner. We never cooked together and rarely ate together. I know it sounds weird, but we were a couple that didn't always act like you'd expect. Plus, he worked weird hours and I have a non-traditional schedule, so we spent a lot of time apart. He would have days off at a time and would go out with his buddies, meet up with girls who he always claimed were "just friends" and he'd go on expensive, frivolous trips. I hated it but he was so good at arguing that I always ended up feeling like the bad guy when I brought up my worries. He was an expert at turning everything around on me."

"I don't mean any offense, but from a bystander's point of view, it really doesn't sound like a good or healthy relationship."

A laugh escaped Sammi's lips and she shook her head while she replied, "I know! I still can't believe I didn't see it. It was like my fear of being alone and my fear of not having anywhere to go blinded me. If we weren't together, who would I be friends with? Where would I live? How would I ever find someone else who would tolerate me and my weird idiosyncrasies? I felt like I was stuck."

"I get it," Camille raised her hand in declaration. "I was in a similar situation once. In law school, I had a boyfriend who I thought was God's gift to the world. He was beautiful, smart, and charming. He was also a cheat, liar, and emotionally abusive. My girlfriends had to spell it out for me. They saw him for what he really was when I couldn't and then, after that I didn't think I would ever find anyone who would love me again. It was so stupid, but we go through these bad breakups, so we know a good relationship when it finds us. Once I met my husband, Max, a light bulb clicked inside my head and I thought back to how stupid and naïve I was when I was with my ex. You can't let those negative thoughts beat you. You can't let them stay with you now. You need to know that there is someone out there for you."

Sammi groaned and dropped her head dramatically into her hands, "I know but I just can't imagine putting myself out there when I live at home with my mom at 35. Ugh, can you say loser?"

She held her left hand up to her forehead while making the letter L with her pointer finger and thumb—a 90's throwback.

Through a large grin, Camille said, "The right guy won't care. And right now, it's not about finding the right guy. It's about focusing on you and getting your life in order."

"You're right, you're exactly right."

Their girl talk moment was broken up when the side door opened and a round man poked his head out.

"Ladies, there's a man here who wants to see Athena. Leash her up and bring her out," Steve demanded with an abrasive snarl.

"Who was that?" asked Camille, as the door slammed shut behind him.

"Steve, the director of the shelter," Sammi said as she shook her head and raised her eyebrows. "He's not known for his kindness. He can be really . . . well, rude, dismissive, abrupt, sort of a dick."

She didn't sugar coat it for her. Her mom had told her stories of Steve and how his attitude and dry nature had turned away many volunteers. Rescue work was incredibly difficult and being the one in charge, making the tough decisions, could harden a person. But the whispers around the shelter said that Steve was already quite difficult before he started working here.

Camille snorted in response, "Sort of a dick . . . I have to agree with that."

They stood up and brushed away the little turf turds that had collected on their hands and pants from sitting on the fake grass with Athena and then took her up front to meet her potential adopter.

As they rounded the corner to the lobby, Camille sucked in her breath like something startled her. She was in the lead, so Sammi didn't understand her star struck reaction until she stepped around the corner and saw the most gorgeous man standing there, waiting for them.

His hazel eyes brightened at the sight of Athena and Camille and Sammi tried not to melt into little puddles on the floor. It took all they had not to stare, or even worse, drool.

Sammi forced her feet to continue their forward movement towards this tall drink of water, so he could meet Athena. Now Camille, who had stopped short, was right on her heels, not wanting to miss a moment of this "crucial learning experience," she explained later.

He dropped from his 6'2" stance to sit on his knees on the hard tile floor when Athena got closer. He held out his strong muscle-bound arm so she could sniff his hand. He talked to her in a gentle, sweet tone that wasn't too loud.

"Hi, pretty girl. I'm Trevor. I saw your photo online and just had to come and meet you."

Camille nudged Sammi in the arm, pushing her forward in the process.

"Uh, hi, so this is Athena. Duh. Um and . . . do you want to go into the room behind you and spend some time with her?"

Very smooth, Sammi thought to herself.

He lifted his eyes to hers and with a smile, stood to walk to the room in question, "Sure."

As soon as his back was towards them, Camille and Sammi looked at each other like two star-stuck teens at their first pop concert. Camille mouthed an over exaggerated, "oh my god" and fanned her face like she was all hot and bothered. Sammi mirrored her enthusiasm but after a few seconds of freaking out, she threw her head back and tried to shake the cobwebs from her brain. This man was H. O. T. and the least she could do in this situation was not make a complete ass of herself.

The ladies hightailed it into the room with Trevor and shut the lower half of the Dutch door, so Athena could be off-leash and the shelter staff could still keep an eye on them—the newbie-volunteers.

Camille stepped up and reached out to shake Trevor's hand, "Hi, I'm Camille. I'm a new volunteer, so I hope it's okay I tag along with Sammi here. This is my first meet-and-greet of a dog and potential adopter, so I have a lot to learn."

"That's cool. It's nice to meet you, Camille. I'm Trevor."

It's very possible her cheeks turned a slight shade of red.

He turned, "You're Sammi? It's nice to meet you. Thanks for bringing Athena in to meet me." He reached his strong hand out to shake.

Sammi's brain stopped short-circuiting for a second and she stumbled into action.

"Yeah, yeah, uh yeah, I'm Sammi," she oh-so eloquently burst into speech as she took in his chiseled features.

He held onto her hand a little longer than normal and she could feel herself not knowing how to react. She just smiled stupidly at him and pulled her hand away when she felt the awkwardness overtaking her.

"So, Athena came in a few months ago as a stray. She was found down by the marina, eating some dead fish and bait from the docked fishing boats. She was super thin, looked to have had puppies recently, and was terrified of the people trying to capture her. She took a long time to warm up to the volunteers here but once she did, she blossomed into a sweet, spunky girl with lots of energy. I think she has a lot of love to give, but she hasn't had anyone show much interest in adopting her yet."

Sammi tried not to ramble, but looking at his dark skin, kind eyes, and athletic build was much easier to do, without being creepy, when she was talking.

"Wow, so she's been here awhile then?"

Trevor was sitting on the ground and Athena was as taken with him as Camille and Sammi. She was standing tall and was leaning into his pets. She even lifted her left paw and offered it to him, which he happily shook and then she inched closer to him, turned her body around and sat down into his side, so they were touching. She was laying it on thick.

Not wanting to drop the bomb that would blow up this possible adoption, Sammi grimaced as she said, "She does need to be in a home without kids and with an owner who is home a lot, because she has some separation anxiety and doesn't do well when she's left alone for a long time, crated or not."

His reaction wasn't one they were expecting.

"No problem," he said without a second thought. "I'm single, don't have any kids, and work from home. Plus, I'm a homebody, so I don't go out much anymore."

Sammi could feel Camille reacting and tried to suppress her urge to happy dance.

"Well, we can let you two get to know each other a little more if you'd like or we can go outside and go for a walk—"

He cut her off, "No need. I made my decision the second she sat down next to me. I'd like to adopt her."

Athena turned and smothered his face in kisses. Those were the words she'd been waiting to hear for many sad months and now they were being said by a beautiful, homebody who worked from home—what a perfect match!

"Okay, I'll let them know at the front desk and they'll call your vet, and references, and if everything checks out, you two will be on your way home soon!" Sammi explained with a stupidly big grin spread across her face.

They left Trevor and Athena alone to bond and informed the staff about his decision to move forward with the adoption. Camille pulled Sammi aside, out of earshot, after they delivered the happy news.

"Ho-ly crap. Girl, it's time to get back on the horse. You have to ask him out!"

"Not a chance in hell," Sammi snorted as she tried not to laugh in her new friend's face. "That man is so far out of my league, he's actually on another planet."

She scoffed back, "He is not! Yeah, he's hot but so are you. He looks to be maybe a few years older than you and let me say, that if I weren't happily married to the most amazing man in the world, I would be asking him out myself! Confidence, girl, confidence!"

"Where were you before? I needed you in my life years ago!" Sammi said, as they both laughed.

A booming voice pulled them from their fun-loving conversation, "Ladies! Once you're done, could you come over here and finish up this adoption?" Steve said in his always present, overly condescending tone.

They scurried over to Athena and Trevor and finalized all the last details and provided him with a leash, purple collar, bag of high-quality dog food, a few toys, and a complimentary Ocean Pals tank top.

They snapped an adoption picture of a smiling Athena and happy, new furdad Trevor that would be posted on the Ocean Pals' Facebook and Instagram pages. Then, everyone said their goodbyes to the beautiful girl who waited so patiently for her forever home.

Sammi leaned down and scratched her chest, "Good luck, pretty girl! I'll miss you so much but I'm so happy you found your forever family. Take good care of him and come back and visit sometime."

She tried to slyly glance up at Trevor with that last statement but was pretty sure it came off as transparent as possible. Oh well, it took Stella a while to get her groove back, right? It'll take Sammi a few tries too.

"Thank you," he said as the shelter staff each took a moment to say their goodbyes to Athena.

"Anytime. Thank you for choosing adoption," Sammi said before Camille chimed in with a question.

"Hey, what do you do for a living? I work from home too and I'm a lawyer."

Before he could answer, the front door opened and JC came flying into the room, late for his shift as always. He was headed straight for the dog side of the building, but he spotted everyone fawning over Athena and Trevor and he spun around to join them with wide eyes.

"Is she going home?" he said, excitement clear in his voice.

"Yup, she's a lucky girl," said Camille as JC kissed Athena on the head and whispered in her ear.

He stood up and finally laid eyes on Trevor as he began to respond to Camille's previous question.

"I have my own accounting business."

JC's eyes just about bulged out of his head when he heard this.

"You're an accountant? Oh my god, I need you . . . I mean, an accountant. I need an accountant for my club. My husband swears and declares I'm going to ruin the books and I would definitely rather hire someone who adopts and supports Ocean Pals, than some rando-person I look up on Google. Do you have a card? Here, I'll just walk you out to your car."

Trevor and JC left just as fast as JC had run into the building and Camille turned to Sammi with a serious look on her face, "He just stole your man!"

Sammi just shook her head and laughed, but a small part of her hoped their paths crossed again.

Chapter 6

BURGER and JC

JC followed Trevor out to his car, chatting away the whole time about his business and financial struggles.

"I just can't cut the budget anymore and I thought I could turn it around with a few more fun events because they always bring in a lot of extra money, but as much as it pains me to say this, Ryan is right. I need some outside help. That copy of *Accounting for Dummies* that I bought just made things worse too. I really think I should be given a refund. It was that bad!"

Trevor turned to face the flustered JC after he helped Athena into his old, beat up Toyota Tacoma.

"I got you. I can help. How about we meet up sometime and go over your books? I'll come to the club and we check things out and make a plan."

"Perfect. Thank you so much. I'll text you the address."

JC leaned into the open window to scratch the top of Athena's head and told her how much he'd miss her and how he's so happy for her.

"Feel free to bring her along whenever we meet. Thanks again!"

Trevor waved and ducked into his car, while JC headed back to the shelter.

He shot off a quick text to Ryan letting him know he scored himself a new accountant, along with a kissy emoji, and a thank you for pushing him in that direction. He always knew what was best.

JC made his way back through shelter and found that no one was walking the dogs. They only got out of their condos for a few minutes a day, so their walks were very important to their mental, physical, and emotional health. He grabbed a leash and brought Burger out to the street for a walk.

Bouncy Burger was an 8-month-old pit-mix who had the energy and cute factor of a puppy but had the basic commands and potty training down pat like an adult. This little sandwich knew how to sit, heel, and give paw already, but he needed an active family to help him expel some of his baby energy. His mostly black fur was spotted with large white patches and his athletic body weighed in at only about 25 pounds. He was what is referred to as a "pocket pittie" for his reduced size.

No one was sure why Burger hadn't been adopted yet. He'd been at the shelter for three months, which was a long time for a young pup like him. He was an owner-surrender who found they "didn't have time for him" once he wasn't a rollie-pollie, little pup anymore. People were the worst sometimes.

JC led the ecstatic pup around the two-block perimeter that walkers followed around the shelter. Burger peed, pooped, sniffed at flowers, and rolled around in the grass and it was clear he was having an absolute ball. How these dogs embraced life to the fullest while being confined to a kennel all day was unbelievable and a true testament to their "enjoy life" attitude.

"Come on, Burger," JC said to the attentive dog when he spotted folks having a drink at the nearby open-air bar, "Let's get you in front of some people!"

Side-by-side the two strutted their way over to Miller's Ale House, where the music was loud, drinks were flowing, and patrons enjoying their happy hour were already aww-ing over the approaching Burger.

JC and Burger hung out for 30 minutes and mingled with everyone at the bar. Many people inquired about Burger, took his picture, and talked about their own dogs. Some even vowed to come adopt him later and even more promised to visit the shelter and check out all the dogs and cats available for adoption.

No one followed them back to the shelter to adopt Burger on the spot, but that might've been good since some of them were a few drinks deep and were getting a little sloppy. JC made sure Burger had enough water and patted him on the head before shutting his condo door. The pup rested on the cool floor, panting and wearing a big smile on his face.

As JC walked back to the lobby to grab a drink from the water fountain, he passed Camille and Sammi in the hall as they were getting ready to leave.

"Ugh, ladies, is there no better feeling than when you make a dog's day?" he gushed with a huge smile on his face. The endorphins from finding an accountant, giving Burger a big walk, and connecting with people possibly interested in adopting had him flying higher than he'd been in a while.

They didn't have time to reply back to him because before he could elaborate, Emily's voice broke through his happy haze.

"JC! Did you take Burger to Miller's without authorization?" she demanded. Her eyes blazed as she moved towards him, fast and aggressive.

"Uh, yeah. We were just walking by and got to talking to a few people. We do it all the time," he explained, while feeling very attacked.

"You're not supposed to take dogs up there without prior permission."

She was pointing her finger at him like he was a child and talked at him like she was in charge.

"Since when? Emily, I've been volunteering here for years and we always walk the dogs up there when people are out drinking. It's a great way to get some free marketing for the dogs and the shelter. People were taking pictures, sending Snapchats to their friends, and posting about Burger on Instagram. He was a freakin' celebrity up there."

"But what if he bites someone or some—"

JC cut her off, "Burger? Bite someone? Are you kidding?"

"No, I'm not kidding. We just can't be going up there and using their facility as our own personal adoption event, okay? Don't do it again."

JC's face contorted into a look that only could be described as the most condescending "yeah, right" look on the planet.

He didn't bother to answer her. He just turned and walked back to the dog run to take another dog out for a walk.

Camille and Sammi clamored back into the dog run with him.

"What was that all about?" asked Camille. "She was all pissed off!"

JC smacked his lips together and shook his head in disgust.

"She's always acting like her shit don't stink, you know? You just have to watch out for her," He explained. "She thinks because she's been volunteering here so long that she can boss us all around. Well, don't forget that she's a volunteer just like we are and she has no authority over us. Don't get me wrong, she knows her shit, but she also has no problem acting like she's Steve's right hand woman. Just don't let her make you feel bad about stuff, okay? Follow the rules they told you about in your orientation and read the handbook and you'll be fine."

He rubbed his hands over his face a few times before he dropped them to his sides.

"We've never had an issue taking the dogs up there before and the owners never fussed about us walking around their parking lot. A friend of mine worked there for a while and she told me they love that we bring the dogs by. They feel like it adds to their cool, laid back atmosphere and they've helped up out with lots of events in the past, so they're a dog-friendly business."

"Have things changed with them?" Sammi asked.

"I don't think so. We walked up there four days ago and no one made a fuss, so I'm just going to ignore her on this one. Thanks for listening to me vent, ladies. I just can't stand her sometimes." He growled the last few words.

"Anytime, JC. "

"Sure, that's what we're here for."

Both ladies replied back, talking over each other. It had been a long day for everyone.

JC waved them off and told them to head home before they got roped into poop duty or even worse, bath duty and they obliged.

He walked up and down the dog corridor and talked to the dogs through the six-foot chain link fence and Dutch doors between them. He stopped at Bianca's door, a silky coated retriever, who was dumped after she couldn't have puppies anymore.

"Come on, good girl. Want to go for a walk?"

She jumped up from her bed, going wild at the "w" word being spoken out loud and directed towards her. Her actions of wiggling, wagging, barking and clawing at her kennel door screamed that, yes, she did want to go for a w-a-l-k and she wanted to go n-o-w.

JC opened the top Dutch door to hook the leash to her collar and then opened the bottom half to let her out once she was secure. The two headed out for a walk and made a beeline right for Miller's Ale House.

"Take that, Emily," JC said to no one, as day-drinkers from Miller's came rushing over to meet Bianca. "Take that."

Chapter 7
BAYLOR and Willa

As Willa walked away from her car, after pulling up to Ocean Pals Shelter, she heard JC call out to her from the street.

"Hey lady! Guess who got adopted today?"

She waited for him to catch up to her and they walked together towards the shelter, along with a gorgeous pittie mix, Navin, who JC had out for his daily walk.

"Who?"

"Athena! Oh my god, she got adopted by this super hot guy who's going to help me with my accounting fiasco at the club. They're a perfect match. I really hope it sticks and she doesn't get brought back."

"Aww yay! But wait, what's going on at the club? Anything I can help with?"

"Oh right, you're a numbers Queen too. I forgot about that. I have been struggling since summer and the tourist season ended. My expenses just seem to be getting higher and higher each month, when all I feel like I'm doing is cutting costs."

"Oh, that sucks. I'm really sorry. Hopefully, this hot accountant can help you figure some things out. We've had some fun nights there," she smiled as she recalled the memories.

"I'll figure it out. I always do."

JC held the front door to the shelter open for her and as she passed by him, she noticed his eyes weren't sparkling like they normally do and his usual positive attitude was forced, while worry lines crinkled around his eyes.

Feeling concern for her friend, Willa watched as JC walked towards the dog run to put Navin back in his condo. She made a mental note to ask him more about his troubles at the club later, but for now, she had to find Emily to let her know she was taking Baylor home for the evening.

Sometimes volunteers would take dogs or cats home for a night, or even a whole weekend, to get to know them better and to give them a break from the lonely shelter life, where it was loud, cold, and they were confined most of the day. It helped break up the monotony and got them out in front of some new eyes, since most volunteers took them on long walks around their neighborhoods or to nearby parks while wearing "Adopt Me" vests.

Baylor, a 9-year-old hound dog, who was dropped off with his canine brother Beetle, wasn't doing well at the shelter. He was depressed, quiet, and confused. He missed his family and Beetle, who had already been adopted without him. He needed a pick me up.

After she found Emily and signed Baylor out for the evening, she loaded him into her SUV and headed home.

When she pulled in the driveway, she saw both of her kids were home. Dalton was supposed to be finishing up his finals at Penn State, so she was surprised to see his car, but Dede was home because her finals were next week and she wanted a quiet place to study. She was majoring in Nursing at the University of Delaware, while Dalton was pursuing a degree in Marketing.

Baylor had a little extra pep in his step now that he was out of the shelter environment. Try all you can to make a shelter a warm, happy place, but it's still tough on the dogs and cats when they don't understand why they're there, why they can't go home, and why they're left alone at night, among other things.

Not acting his age of nine, Baylor practically bounced through the front door of Willa's bay front bungalow. She called out to her kids that she was home and had a special visitor with her when Dede came around the corner with a serious look on her face.

Willa's stomach dropped and fear coursed through her veins, "What's wrong?"

"I don't know, but something is going on with Dalton. He showed up a few minutes ago and when I asked why he wasn't in school for finals, he just said it doesn't matter and then mumbled something like, "I can't, I quit" and practically dragged himself up to his room. I followed him, but he slammed the door and locked me out. Mom, he's acting weird. Like, super sad and . . . his eyes, they're almost hollow, like he didn't really look at me. I was about to call you."

The pit in Willa's stomach grew as she listened to her daughter explain the situation. It sounded eerily familiar and her heart ached knowing what it could be and what her son was experiencing.

"Your dad had episodes like this when he was Dalton's age. He still does sometimes, but he's on medication . . . or at least he was last time we were together."

Dede just looked at her with wide eyes and Willa felt a surge of guilt. She should have talked to her kids about this sooner, but now wasn't the time to dwell on that. They needed to act and help Dalton.

"Dede, your dad has been living with depression and anxiety his whole life. It sounds like Dalton might be experiencing it too."

Willa left a stunned Dede in the foyer with Baylor while she rushed to Dalton's room. She knocked on his door and yelled into him.

"Dalton, it's your mom. Can I come in please? I'd like to talk."

"Go away, Mom. I just want to sleep."

"Please, let me in. I'll be quick, just a few minutes. I haven't seen you since summer break and want to say hi."

No answer.

She tried the doorknob, which was still locked, and then leaned into the door to try and pop it open since the saltwater air sometimes made the doors expand outside their hardware and not shut right. No luck there either.

Panic started to set in. She just wanted to see him and make sure he was okay. She knew he asked for some space, and maybe she should accept that and provide him some, but this was her son and her mind raced with overwhelming fear and worry.

Space be damned.

An idea jolted her into action and she called out to Dede, "Bring Baylor here."

She knocked again when the hound dog was by her side, tail wagging and ready for anything.

"Dalton, I brought home a dog you might want to meet. His name is Baylor. He's available for adoption at Ocean Pals but I brought him here because he's struggling at the shelter. His old owners dumped him there after nine years together because they wanted to get a puppy and didn't think the older dogs would be able to handle it. His brother, Beetle, already got adopted so he's stuck in the shelter alone. He has arthritis, goopy eyes, and some lumps and bumps, but his tail is wagging hard out here and I think he wants to meet you."

Dalton had a soft spot for older dogs. Ever since he was young, he gravitated towards them and said he enjoyed their old souls who knew how to love so deeply. Dalton was the reason Willa got into rescue in the first place. He volunteered with the shelter in middle school for an extra credit assignment. He always advocated for rescue dogs and cats and was hoping to use his marketing degree to work in a shelter or vet's office in the future.

When no sound of movement came from his room, Willa was about to give up and go find a screwdriver to take to the door lock but then Baylor acted instead. He barked, and then barked again, and again and scratched at the door like a puppy trying to break in. That's not like him. He was normally very calm and quiet and Willa wasn't sure she had ever heard him bark before, but he was causing a raucous now and his hound dog bay and loud bark must've gotten Dalton's attention, because the door clicked and slowly opened.

When Willa saw Dalton, she flashed back to her first encounter with Thomas's depression when they were just dating. First off, he looked so much like his father normally and now, it was almost a mirror image of her former husband when he was only her boyfriend and she showed up to his apartment for a date and he answered the door looking deeply pained and jittering from anxiety.

Willa had spent the night with him, where she rubbed his hair and listened to his worries that flowed relentlessly from his mouth. Luckily, she was able to get him to agree to see a counselor and get help, but it took some time and almost ended their relationship. Once Thomas got help and found the right medication for his depression and anxiety, he had many fewer attacks and was able to live alongside his mental health struggles.

Dalton's eyes were dark and red from tears, but they fixated on Baylor as soon as the door opened and he dropped his body to the floor and the dog swarmed into his arms. Dalton buried his face into Baylor's white and brown fur and his body heaved with waves of sobs. Baylor stood in his arms and draped his head over the young man's shoulder, as if he was hugging him back.

Willa felt her heart break and seize in tandem. Her heart broke for the pain Dalton was in, the emotions pouring out of him were raw, but it seized for the immediate and amazing bond her son and adoptable Baylor had just created.

This dog who never met Dalton before felt his emotions and need for a friend through the closed door and put himself into a situation to comfort without a second thought. And this was a dog a family was willing to abandon and give up on just because he was old. People really fucking sucked.

Dalton pulled his face away from Baylor and looked up at Willa, who sat down next to the hugging pair.

"Mom," his voice creaked, "I don't know what's going on, but I can't shake this feeling . . . of dread or like something bad is going to happen. I can't explain it. One day I woke up and there it was, like a sad, little bird sitting on my shoulder. It followed me around all day and I tried to ignore it, but it just got worse and worse. It made me think thoughts I'd never consider before and had me worrying about stuff I never even thought of until now."

The words flowed out of him like a rushing river as he spoke to her through his sobs.

"The next day, it was worse and I had this lump in my throat all the time, so I never felt like eating. I thought I had a cold or something, but it never went away and then I just got sleepy and couldn't bring myself to get out of bed. I didn't go to class for weeks and my roommates tried to cover for me, but they have their own stuff to deal with and I didn't take my finals, so now I won't graduate on time, but Mom . . . Mom, I don't even care. I just don't care about anything and feel like I could crawl into a hole and die and it wouldn't matter."

He looked at her with such pain, confusion, and heartache. Her whole body ached to make this better and to make it go away, but she knew it was going to take time. So, she let her own tears flow and reached out to grab her son's hand.

"Oh sweetie, we'll get you help. I promise you won't always feel like this. I'm here for you and I love you and I'll do whatever it takes to get you feeling better."

The next morning, Willa pulled her tired body from Dalton's floor, where she slept, to go make some coffee. Once it was brewed, she poured herself a cup, threw on a sweater, and walked out to the wraparound deck to finalize her plan. She couldn't sleep, so she researched psychiatrists on her phone all night while Baylor spooned Dalton in his bed.

She pulled the salty air into her lungs and closed her eyes, listening to the water lap against the dock. This was her happy place but right now, it wasn't doing much to ease her mind. First, she had to call Thomas and fill him in on the night's details, which she did with some reservation. He answered on the first ring and vowed to jump in his car and drive over immediately, but Willa talked him down.

"Let's give him a little space this morning. I'll wait until he wakes up and then I'll talk to him about therapy. You two still aren't on great terms, but maybe you can reach out to him this afternoon and see if he's interested in talking or meeting up."

Thomas wasn't happy about her suggestion but agreed to go along with it since he knew Dalton was still pissed at him for his infidelity years ago.

After she got off the phone with Thomas, she made a few calls to some local therapists to schedule an appointment. Once done with her calls, she checked in on Dede's room, where she was already up and studying. Always the amazing and motivated student, Willa wasn't surprised to find Dede sitting in bed, surrounded by all her books, notes, laptop, and tablet. Willa got her a fresh cup of coffee, pulled her into a big hug, and let her get back to her studying, with the promise of pancakes later.

From her daughter's room, she grabbed another cup of coffee and poked her head into Dalton's room. He was awake and rubbing Baylor's big, soft hound dog ears while he got intermittent kisses from the gentle, senior dog.

"Hey, sweetie," she said softly as she placed his steaming coffee mug on his wooden bedside table.

"Hey, Mom," he whispered, emotion still evident in his voice.

They sat in silence for a few minutes, their bodies enveloped by the painful atmosphere of the room.

"I think I need some help."

Dalton's voice was small, almost weak, but Willa was so thrilled and proud to hear those six words. She would move heaven and earth to get him help.

"I do too. I already made some calls this morning and, if it's okay with you, I made a 2 p.m. appointment for you to talk to a therapist in town."

He nodded his head, as tears flowed down his soft cheeks. "Thank you," he whispered again. "Thank you."

Chapter 8

TILLY and Camille

"Here kitty, kitty," mewed Camille, "Come on, sweet baby. I'll give you some love."

She was trying to encourage a small black and white cat out of hiding, while she played with and dodged the tiny, razor-sharp claws of three other kittens frolicking around her.

The green-eyed feline slowly crept out from under the large cat-scratching tree to sniff the treats Camille had thrown her way. She had been working on making friends with this kitty for 30 minutes and this was the first sign of movement in her direction.

The other kittens had no fear of her and climbed all over her lap and body as she sat on the cool tile floor of the shelter's cat room. They meowed the littlest meows and scrunched up their tiny faces when they had something to say, but always the curious little creatures, they explored every inch of Camille and the cat room and used their claws to grab, pull, and balance their way through every obstacle.

It took another 15 minutes to coax the scared cat towards her, but she was patient and finally successful when the kitty ate all the treats Camille could hold. Once she got a taste of one, it was like the flood gates opened and she couldn't woof them down fast enough. Camille spent another 15 minutes petting her and talking to her in hopes to get her more used to people, so she'd be more adoptable.

Once she had her fill of claw marks and felt she made an impact on the fearful kitty, she decided to go visit the dog run area and check on the laundry situation. But she stopped in her tracks when a man came into the shelter lobby pulling a black and white shepherd mix behind him.

"I need you to take her," the man barked at Emily, who was manning the front desk.

"Okay, sir. First, what's going on? Why do you need to surrender her and what's her name?"

Emily was calm and didn't bat an eye at the man's aggressive tone or the fact that he was planning to dump his older dog, who looked about as terrified as could be. Camille watched from the back edge of the reception area, mostly because she wanted to see what was going to happen, but also because she would have had to cross right through the area where the current, uncomfortable situation was going down.

"I'm moving in with my girlfriend and she doesn't like her. If I can't get rid of her today, I'll have to take her to the vet and have her put down."

"Has she ever bitten anyone? Is she good with other dogs? Kids? Cats? Has she had vet care?" Emily spouted off a list of questions to the man.

"No, she never bit anyone and she's good with everyone and all animals." His voice softened a bit. "She hasn't been to the vet in a few years, but she's a great dog, so I don't want to have to put her to sleep."

Camille restrained herself from busting into the conversation. How could this man be willing to kill his own dog because of his girlfriend? She wanted to ask him so many questions to try and understand his reasoning and thought process. She wanted to argue with him and to explain how shitty it was that he'd abandon her and worse, be willing to kill her just because of some new flame. But, she held back. This wasn't her fight to fight. She needed to learn and hopefully, could be an advocate for these animals later, when she knew how the animal rescue world worked.

Emily's back tightened and her voice had a new edge to it that it didn't before.

"Sir, fill out this form and we'll take her. A donation is appreciated."

While the man filled out the forms, Emily turned to Camille and made an annoyed face expressing her disgust for him and this situation. Then she asked Camille if she could take the now homeless dog to the back, where Zak would administer some shots and do her intake exam.

Camille jumped to action. "Sure, will do."

When Camille approached her, the mature girl cowered towards her owner, but he just handed Camille the leash and stepped farther away from his dog.

"What's her name?" Camille asked, as her heart broke for the poor pup.

"Tilly." He grunted as he shoved the forms back to Emily with a $20 bill. Then he turned and walked out without another look back at his terrified dog.

Tilly's eyes followed her owner out the door and she pulled hard towards him, but Camille held her back. She whined a painful cry and stared at the door, waiting and wishing for him to return.

Tears welled up in Camille's eyes as she fought to keep her emotions at bay. The lump in her throat made it hard to speak but she forced the words out.

"Tilly, sweetie. Come here, girl. You're safe now. We'll find you a new home, a better home. One that will take care of you forever. Come here, sweetie, come on, Tilly."

The dog turned her head and looked towards Camille, almost like she was questioning herself on whether or not she should listen to this new woman holding her leash.

Camille continued to talk softly to the terrified dog, who finally gave in and after one last look towards the front door, turned and pressed her body into Camille's open arms.

Getting Tilly to the exam room was another story. She didn't walk nicely beside Camille to the room, nor did she pull on the leash, in fact she didn't walk there at all. Once the brevity of the situation dawned on her and the loud sounds and harsh smells of the shelter got to her, Tilly decided she wasn't going anywhere with anyone.

She plopped down on the floor and refused to move from her spot in the shelter lobby. Camille tried to lure her with treats, encouraged her with a fun, happy voice, and she even got down on all fours and showed her the way, but Tilly refused and Camille had to call in for backup.

She asked Zak for help, the shelter's best employee. He was only 23 years old, but he had a great work ethic and supreme knowledge of dog behavior and training. They were lucky to have him on staff.

She and Zak had to physically move Tilly to the exam room and the easiest way to do that was for Camille to push her butt and Zak to guide her front half through the small lobby and past the door to the vet care area.

Tilly took this move well but was still very scared. She never showed any signs of aggression or acted like she was going to lash out from fear, but she shook like a leaf and her eyes looked about as sad as could be. The middle-aged girl had given up.

Once Tilly was done with her exam and shots, Camille and Zak set her up in a condo on the adoptable dog side with a bed, blanket, bowl of water, and a chew toy. Closing the door to her kennel was soul crushing.

Camille locked eyes with the sweet girl and explained that everything would be okay and that she knew she was scared but promised to help find her a forever home. It didn't help either of them feel any better though. Tilly's rejection and abandonment from her owner broke her heart and she was mourning the loss of her old life and freedom.

The loud barks and howls of the other dogs made her flinch and she watched Camille's every move as she shut her gate and moved to walk away. Her eyes screamed, "Stay. Help me. Save me," as she jumped on the closed door and barked towards Camille, who turned and walked away, brushing her tears from her cheeks as she went.

Camille went straight to the laundry room and buried her head in her hands. She let the tears flow and her body ached in sorrow for Tilly and the thousands of homeless dogs every day, all over the world. The pain she felt was nothing compared to what they were going through, but in that moment—that moment of feeling like she needed to be able to do more, to help more, and to do her small part to make the world a better place—she vowed to step up her volunteer game and put her skills and connections to work.

"You okay?" asked Zak when he walked into the small laundry room and found Camille wiping away the last of her tears.

"Uh, yeah, I guess. It's just hard." She took a deep breath. "Tilly was so sad and she's so broken. How do you deal with that every day?"

Zak half shrugged and released a breath before answering, "You just sort of have to. I try to focus on the good stuff and the good parts of rescue when shit like that happens. And that kind of intake doesn't happen every day, but the dogs are always scared when they come in and are dropped off. But they quickly adapt to our routine and realize that we're nice and are here to help them, and that we play with them and love them. Every day, they come out of their shell a little more. You'll see it the longer you're here. One day, a dog will be shut down and won't come out of their kennel for any reason. They'll piss and shit all over themselves, but we keep working with them and we give them baths, talk quietly to them, offer them treats, and give them encouragement and love. Then the next week, you'll find them out in the yard, playing, running, and loving on you instead. It's a process. Sometimes, you have to be really patient and it takes dogs weeks on weeks to chill out but other times, it's like a flip of a switch—they just get over it and move on. Plus, seeing them find their forever home makes it all worth it. You gotta focus on the positives. The first time they walk on a leash, or wag their tail, or seek out your attention—whatever it is, those moments keep me going."

Camille nodded, "That makes sense. I'll have to work on that. You're doing great work here, Zak. Thank you."

He looked at her somewhat surprised and then serious, "Thank you. I really appreciate that. It's nice to hear."

He gave her arm a squeeze and sauntered off to tackle another chore that needed done, leaving Camille alone in the laundry room. She wiped her face a few more times to dry her tear-stained cheeks and headed out to the front reception area to talk to Emily. She needed as much information on how to deal with the high-stress, high-emotion atmosphere of the shelter and wanted to tap into the best resources out there—the long-term volunteers and employees.

"Hey, Emily," Camille said as she leaned against the front desk, "How did you keep your cool with that asshat who brought Tilly in earlier?"

Emily rolled her eyes at the memory of the man and said, "Yeah. It's something I've had to work on for a long time . . . to not tear the people who come in here, demanding we take their dogs or cats, a new one. I want to scream at them but over the years I've learned, it doesn't matter. They've already made the decision to drop their animal off, to abandon it, and move on. There's nothing I can say that would make them change their minds and then, for them give that animal the life it deserves. If we chase them away and don't take their pet, they might have it euthanized at the vet, let it loose in the middle of nowhere, take it to a high kill-shelter, or worse, shoot it themselves."

As she heard of this sad reality, Camille's eyes widened in shock.

"Right, so that's why I just get as much basic information as I can and get them on their way. Because we want to save the animals and we want to help them heal and find new homes. We have to be a resource for people here if we want them to do what's best for the dogs and cats. My personal opinion on what they're doing is never going to stop them or help our cause, so I just keep my mouth shut as best I can and do everything in my power to help the animals that come through our doors."

Camille nodded in agreement, "Wow. Yeah, I never thought about it like that before. My first reaction was to, well, react but I . . . really see where you're coming from and the logical side of my brain agrees with you, 1,000% percent. The emotional side of my brain gets it too, but it's more hesitant . . . and it wants to yell at people."

They both let out a laugh and Camille felt her shoulders release as some of the tension stuck in her body faded away. She needed that laugh and made a mental note to remember that in the future. Laughter really could be the best medicine.

When she finally got ready to leave for the day, she passed Zak talking to a pretty, college-aged woman in the lobby. She looked familiar, but Camille couldn't place her. Zak was actually smiling, something he didn't do a lot of, and was very engaged in the conversation. Camille decided to say bye to the cats before she left and popped into the cat room for a minute to hand out treats, give a few chin scratches, and to remind everyone to be nice to each other. The kitties could get a little wild at night and without supervision, from time to time, the staff would come in to find their room a mess, toys everywhere, and scratch marks drawn across their tiny ears or faces.

With her goodbyes complete, she turned to actually leave this time but was stopped by Emily and Zak on her way out.

"Guess who just got adopted?" Emily taunted.

"Who? Who?" Camille probed.

"Baylor!" Emily cheered.

"Aww, that's wonderful! Was it that girl Zak was just talking to who adopted him?"

Zak chimed in, "No, well, sort of. That was Willa's daughter, Dede, and she came in to drop off some supplies they had because they were only going to keep Baylor overnight for a few days, but instead decided to keep him forever. I guess he really bonded with Willa's son."

Camille clapped her hands together and felt a huge smile spread across her face. The good news in the shelter world really did help squash the sad stuff.

Zak's face held a sly smile, like he had a secret.

"What?" Camille asked, eyeing him curiously.

He held his hands out in a flourish and with a twinkle in his eye said, "I also got her number."

And with that, he backed away from the two ladies and danced his way back to work.

At home, Camille couldn't help but talk about her day at the shelter over dinner. She explained to her son, Damien, and her husband, Max, how Tilly was brought in and how helpless she felt. She also explained her excitement and joy when she found out Baylor was adopted. The rollercoaster of emotions really took her for a ride today and she told them both that she wanted to do more, help more, and make a difference.

"Babe, wow. That's wonderful. I'm glad you're loving volunteering with the dogs and cats, but are you sure you have time to do more? Are you worried about your emotional health at all? It seems like a lot and I know you can handle it, but I also worry," Max explained as they all sat around the table finishing up their baked ziti and salad dinner.

"I know it's a lot Max, but I love it and even though it's hard sometimes, at the end of the day, I really feel accomplished and like I did something that mattered."

"What about your work? You had been talking about going back to full-time with your law practice."

"I know, and while I love my work, I don't want to take on more divorce cases or real estate settlement work when I could be doing something more powerful and rewarding at the shelter. And yes, I'll be giving up good money to volunteer, but I wouldn't give up my practice completely. I still want to be involved with the law."

Max, always the supportive husband and not one to ever bring more conflict into his life, smiled at his wife, "We don't need the money, babe. We're fine in that department, so if this is what you want to do, I say go for it. Just be careful that it doesn't become too emotionally draining. That's my one caveat . . . my one ask of you."

"Deal."

Camille couldn't help but smile as a thought popped into her head.

"One more thing, Max," she smiled sweetly at him, giving him her best "I love you and need something from you" eyes.

"Oh boy . . ." he laughed.

"Do you think the school would be interested in doing a fundraiser for the shelter? Like a donation drive or something? Maybe have some of the kids come visit and do some volunteer hours?"

He paused for a few beats and then said, "I don't see why not. See if the shelter would be interested first before I take it to the school board."

"Okay, sounds good. Thank you. You're the best husband ever," she said to him with a tilt of her head as she placed her hand on top of his.

He nodded and gave her a wink, "I know."

They gazed into each other's eyes for a few more seconds while Camille slowly bit her lower lip and Max rubbed his thumb along her intertwined hand.

"Uh, guys, stop," Damien pleaded with a disgusted look on his face. "Don't be gross . . . or at least wait until I'm out of the room."

He rolled his eyes at his parents as they laughed and pulled their hands back to themselves.

"Mom, did Caleb find a home yet?"

Damien was referring to the stray dog he found one day at the park a few months ago. He demanded they take him to a no-kill shelter and that's how Camille ended up volunteering for Ocean Pals in the first place. He asked about Caleb every week, always hopeful the stray dog was finally in his forever home.

"Not yet, sweetie, but I walked him today and he was a very good boy. The right family will come for him. It might take some time though."

"I know, I just want him . . . to be . . . to be in his forever home. To not have to sleep alone in the shelter at night, you know?"

Camille nodded in agreement, wholeheartedly understanding what her son was feeling.

"Since you're going to be at the shelter more, maybe I can help out sometimes too?" he asked cautiously. "That lady said 12-year-olds can help at events. I want to do that, Mom. Can you find out if they need anyone else for their next few events? And . . . maybe you could hook it up so that I could hang with Caleb? So I can see him again."

The hopeful, almost puppy dog look on his face sealed the deal and Camille agreed to ask around and sign him up as a teen volunteer for the next event.

"What 12-year-old boy wants to spend time volunteering and helping others?" She asked Max later before they went to bed.

He leaned over to give her one last kiss before he smiled and replied, "Really special ones I guess."

Chapter 9

NAVIN and Steve

Steve nervously picked at a crack in the table while his eyes darted around the room, waiting for a familiar, yet menacing face to appear. The small dining room, of this hole-in-the-wall restaurant, always gave him the creeps but it's where Chris demanded they meet. Every month, Steve made up an excuse to leave the shelter early and he drove down US-113 South to Snow Hill to see his bookie.

Just like last month and the month before that, he showed up empty handed. All the money he had re-allocated from the shelter burned a hole in his pocket and he ended up at the casino off Racetrack Road in Berlin. He promised himself he wouldn't spend it all and that he would just play a hand or two at the poker table, but one hand always led to another, and another, and soon enough, he lost all the money he had stolen in the first place.

Now three-months past due on the loan he took from Chris, the knots in his stomach cramped tighter as he waited to pass along the bad news. Chris had already warned him this was the last time he'd let him skate without paying up, but with the holidays fast approaching, the shelter would be getting a crap-ton of extra donations from those feeling generous over the holidays and he calculated he could pay him back his entire amount, plus interest.

The door chimed and Steve snapped his head around. When he saw who it was, his stomach sank and spasmed in his body that was already all frazzled and shaky. Chris moseyed through the scattered four-top tables and roughly pulled out a chair, across from Steve, spun it around, and straddled it, so he could rest his arms on the back rest.

"You got it?" he asked, his voice bristly.

Always one to skip formalities, he got right to the point, even though Steve could've used a few extra minutes to swallow the lump lodged in his throat.

"No, but I'll have it soon," the words rushed out of his mouth and sounded more pathetic than planned. "The holidays bring in lots of extra money for the shelter and I—"

His words trailed off as Chris held up his thick hand, signaling him to stop.

Chris's face was meaner and more contorted than normal. His stubble was thick as he pulled his lips into a nasty frown and his eyes looked like they could spout fire as he opened his mouth to speak.

"This was your last chance. You promised the money this time."

"I know, I know, but I truly mean it this time. I promise I'll ha—" Steve stammered.

"Your promises mean nothing to me."

"This time is different. You don't understand. I have a plan and I'll bring double next month. Just give me another month man, please," Steve begged.

"I have a plan too. You better watch out. Life just got a lot more complicated for you."

Chris's words rang in Steve's ear and left a pit of fear in their wake. He turned to explain again and to ask for forgiveness, but Chris was already up and out the door—most likely on the phone with a colleague laughing about how they could make Steve's messy life even more miserable.

Back at the shelter, Steve replayed Chris's words over and over in his head. His threatening message left Steve with no choice but to come up with the money as soon as possible. So, with shaking hands, he logged into the shelter's bank accounts and started transferring small amounts of money to the miscellaneous fund, which was a cover for his gambling debts. He then transferred that money to his secret personal account, which was hidden from his wife, and opened under a fake name.

Once he had some money moved from the shelter's accounts to his private bank account, he texted Chris that he had some of the money now and would work on getting him another $25,000 next week. As he stood up and stretched, he hoped the money would be enough to appease Chris and keep him from doing anything rash.

He saw Navin come back from a walk with a volunteer and asked the woman to bring him into his office. Steve would often have a cat or dog in there with him while he worked. It gave the animal a little time out of their condo and in return, they helped Steve relax while he worked on the stressful task of "adjusting" the shelter's finances and masking his embezzlement scheme.

Navin bounced into his small office, full of energy even though he just had a 30-minute walk. His golden fur didn't shine like it should and Steve made a note to adjust his food to a mixture of dry and wet, instead of just hard kibble. He wanted Navin to look his best for potential adopters since the poor, pocket pittie had been returned twice so far. Navin's only flaw was that he had a lot of energy and they've had trouble finding the right family for him, one that could harness his excitement and vitality for life.

The 40-pound dog was a typical pittie, with muscular legs, a strong chest, and wide face, but he was smaller in height, hence the pocket pittie name. Navin had the normal pitbull personality too— sweet, loving, smart, and misunderstood. He wanted to be your best friend and constant companion, not a vicious, guard dog that some people expected him, and his breed, to be.

Navin popped his front legs up onto Steve's chair as he rubbed the dog's ears and face. Steve asked the volunteer to shut his office door after she dropped Navin off and now, behind that closed door, he softly explained to Navin the serious and dangerous trouble he had gotten himself in.

After he told the handsome dog his woes, Navin covered his face in kisses and offered Steve his paw. Steve smiled sadly at him, feeling a twinge of guilt for stealing money allotted for special dogs like him. So, to quash that guilt, he pulled open his side desk drawer and gave the pup a few treats. He ate them up gratefully and then dropped his paws from Steve's chair, sat on his haunches like a good boy, lifted his wide head, and pulled his lips back, showing off his shiny white teeth. Navin and his big boy smile.

You gotta love this boy, Steve thought as he fished around his desk and gave him a few more treats.

A knock on his door brought Steve back to real life after he had spent the last few hours with his head buried in the shelter's finances. He continued to move money around from different accounts and he wrote down what each transfer was "supposedly" for, so he could make note of them in the shelter's QuickBooks ledger. He had authority over the accounts, but since the shelter was a non-profit, he gave quarterly meetings to the board of directors and they liked to review the shelter's finances. Steve was good enough at cooking the books to keep the wool pulled over their eyes, but he did have an accomplice that helped keep his secret.

The knock on the door also woke up Navin, who was snoozing on the dog bed along the back corner of the wall. He shot up and wiggled his whole body when he saw that it was Emily who poked her head in the door. Emily dropped to her knees and greeted Navin with lots of ear scratches, kisses, and positive affirmations, like "Who's a good boy?" and "Oh, you're so handsome!"

"What's up?" Steve asked as he rubbed his tired eyes.

"I'm about to head out. I'll put Navin back in his condo, so you can just lock up and leave when you're done."

"Sounds good, thanks, Em. You're a real lifesaver."

He winked at Emily, who just smiled back before she clipped a leash to Navin's collar and returned to the dog kennels to put him to bed for the night.

Steve heard the chaos of all the dog's barking and clamoring for Emily's attention as she put Navin back in his condo, but they all calmed down after a few minutes once she turned the lights off and left for the day. The soft sounds of classical music playing soothed the dogs to sleep and that's the last thing Steve heard before everything went dark.

Chapter 10

HOLLYWOOD, CALEB, Willa & Camille

Willa poured herself a giant cup of coffee, into her travel mug, before she yelled out to her kids that she was leaving. She got a grunt and a barely audible, "okay, bye" in response from her kids and a woof from Baylor, their new dog.

Well, at least he cares enough to give me a proper send off, she thought to herself as she grabbed her purse and walked out to her car.

They only adopted Baylor a few weeks ago but it felt like he had been a part of their lives forever. The hound dog went everywhere with Dalton, her oldest son, who was in the midst of battling a knock-down-drag-out fight with his depression and anxiety. Baylor's presence helped calm Dalton and gave him someone to talk to, other than his mom, sister, or therapist. His therapist even suggested they look into getting Baylor certified as an "Emotional Support Animal" since he's had such a profound effect on Dalton's mental health.

Dalton was doing a little better but was nowhere near out of the woods. He would be battling his depression and anxiety for the rest of his life, but he was on the right path to finding a good balance of therapy, medication, and support for the time being. He also mended the fence somewhat with his father, Willa's ex, Thomas, who cheated on her for years, which caused a major rift between him and his son. Thomas also battles with depression and his knowledge, guidance, and understanding has helped bridge the gap for the former estranged son and father.

Willa finally felt somewhat back to normal after the last few, crazy weeks. Between the busyness of the upcoming holiday season, her volunteer efforts at the shelter, helping Dalton manage his mental health struggles, plus playing referee with him and Thomas, and coordinating moving Dede back home for winter break, her plate was over flowingly full. In fact, she felt like she had enough for two plates . . . maybe even a whole dining set. Oh, and did she mention that her baby, Dede, was dating Zak from the shelter?

Ugh.

Her drive to Ocean Pals was uneventful, something she was thankful for, and when she saw

Camille getting out of her car as she pulled up, she honked her horn and felt a smile pull at her cheeks. She really liked Camille and the two had a lot of shifts together, so they were getting to know each other and were becoming fast friends.

Camille waved and stood on the sidewalk to wait for Willa to park so they could walk into the shelter together. They had the early morning shift today, which meant they were the first ones to arrive, so they opened the shelter, fed the dogs and cats, cleaned up their condos and kitty rooms, and changed out all their bedding. They'd also make a list of all the dogs that needed baths, would start the laundry cycle for the day, and checked in on the animals on the recovery side that were healing from illness or surgery. Once all that was done, they'd start rotating the dogs, one by one from their condos, so they could go out into the small yard area to pee and stretch their legs.

The shelter wouldn't open to the public until 11 a.m. and since it was barely 8, they had a few hours to themselves before any potential adopters came to look around.

"Hey hey! How are you doing this fine morning?" Camille asked as she got out of her car. Her bright and cheery disposition contrasted that of Willa's tired, moody one.

"My coffee hasn't kicked in yet," Willa replied, her mood evident.

"Ohh boy, I see someone isn't a morning person."

Willa smiled at her friend, then scrunched her face up at her, and stuck her tongue out for good measure.

"Very mature," Camille laughed as the two hugged and then walked towards the shelter together.

"How are things going at home?" Camille asked, her voice soft with understanding.

Willa had been filling her in on the happenings in her home life and found Camille to be an excellent listener and sounding board, who gave smart advice and lifted her up with encouraging words when she needed them.

"Okay. Dalton is in therapy twice a week and he said his medication seems to be helping. He still hangs in his room a lot but has been getting out more with Baylor. They take long walks together and I think that outside time is good for him. He always comes back with a little more pep in his step. He did mention going back to school for the first time since he got home. We're thinking maybe online classes might be best for now, but we'll see. I'd like to see him take it slow."

Camille nodded but stayed silent as Willa continued.

"Dede is home for winter break. She aced all her finals, which is typical for her . . . but what isn't typical is how much time she's been spending with Zak."

Camille's head whipped around and her eyes widened in surprise.

"You know they went on a date, right?" Willa asked.

"Yeah, I knew that and I was there when he got her number. He was really into her, I think. I just didn't know it had gone beyond that one date."

"Oh my gosh, yes. They're practically connected at the hip and that's not like Dede. She's furiously independent, always has been, but she's fallen hard for our dear boy Zak."

"And . . . judging by your tone . . . you . . . aren't sure about them together now?" Camille asked, her inquisitive spidey-sense kicking in.

"Not unsure, but not sure. I just don't want her getting in over her head, you know? He's a few years older than her and while that isn't a big deal, it is when she's 19 and he's 23. I sat him down and asked him to be careful with her and she and I've had the whole "Sex is a big step" talk, but I just . . . I don't know."

"Is she on birth control?"

"Yeah, but it's more than that. I just don't want her getting hurt. She's only home for a few weeks and then she goes back to UDub, where her class load is enormous and she's up for this part-time internship at a doctor's office. Where in there will she have time for a long-distance boyfriend? It just seems like a recipe for disaster, but she doesn't want to listen to her old fart mom who "just doesn't get it." Willa used air quotes over the last few words and drew them out in her best annoyed-teenage girl voice.

Camille chuckled and patted her friend on the back.

"Ohhh Willa, it'll be fine. Like you said, she's a smart girl. She's gotta figure it out on her own. Let her take a risk with her heart and see where it takes her. Better now, with someone you know, than when she's at school and you have no clue what's going on."

Willa shrugged and dropped her head back in defeat.

"Ugh, I knowwwww."

The ladies were laughing as they walked up the sidewalk and turned the corner to unlock the shelter door, but both stopped suddenly when they saw what was in front of them. The front door was damaged and hanging wide open. A screwdriver hung from the lock and spray paint stretched from the top of the door onto the building.

Willa rushed inside as Camille followed behind and dug in her purse for her phone. She called 911 as they stared in astonishment at the state of the building. The reception desk had been trashed. Papers were everywhere, supplies had been thrown around the room, and it looked like someone had a taken a sledgehammer to the top of the desk. Steve's office door was open, which was unusual since he locked it every evening before he left. His desk looked similar to that of the reception desk, but his computer was in pieces on the floor. Camille finished her frantic call with 911 and let Willa know the police were on their way when she saw that someone had thrown a chair through the large glass window that led to the kitty room.

Panic-stricken and even more upset than before, she ran to the cat room and assessed the damage. Glass was strewn all over the floor and a few of the cat trees were broken, like someone had picked them up over their heads and smashed them into the ground. Spray paint covered the formerly freshly painted concrete walls with doodles, curse words, and inappropriate, violent images.

Camille felt a wave of relief wash over her as she saw that none of the cats were released from their cages. They all were there and accounted for, even though they were cowered together in the corners of their cages, finding strength together after the overnight ordeal. The shattered glass seemed to have spared them and only a few pieces got into their cages, but all the kitties would have to be thoroughly checked out by a vet later. No blood was visible, so that was a good sign.

"All the cats are here and still in their cages," Camille called out to Willa.

"Come in here . . . now!"

The tone of Willa's voice shook Camille to the core and she took off running towards the dog's condos. She busted through the doors and found Willa cradling Hollywood, a 155-pound Great Dane, whose mostly black fur shined except for the four-white fur-socks he wore on his tippy toes.

Camille stood frozen and shock radiated through her body. She couldn't move or begin to believe the sight before her eyes.

Hollywood had a gash on his back thigh, where dried blood had pooled around his hind end. He was awake, but out of it, and there was another slash on his head and ear, which Willa examined as she stroked his fur and told him it would be okay. The doors to his condo were open and dented from the inside, like he had pushed them open with his six-foot tall frame.

Willa's eyes met Camille's and fear, anger, and bewilderment clouded her normally composed vision.

"Who would do this?" she cried, emotion dripping from her voice.

Camille didn't answer because she finally jumped to action and frantically checked all the other dogs and their kennels. Most were fine and were barking wildly like they always do, but an open kennel door in the back caught her eye and dread coursed through her veins. Her stomach dropped so far it was near her knees, but she pushed through her emotions and launched herself back to the open kennel.

Her heart broke as she saw Caleb lying on his side, blood dripping from his mouth and front paws. His tail wagged when he saw her but he didn't move. She clamored to him and fell on her knees at his side. Her hands shook as she held them over his torn skin. She talked to him through her tears, telling him help was one the way and that she'd get him through this. She looked around his kennel as she talked and saw one of his big teeth lying on the floor near the door. He was holding his front, left paw at an awkward angle and she saw another cut on his back. Thankfully, it wasn't bleeding anymore.

The two ladies stayed with the injured dogs and whispered to them through their tears as sirens wailed in the distance. Their emotions flowed freely as they watched as officers swarmed the building and checked for the violent culprits of this crime. Once they cleared the area, a detective came in and spoke to Willa and Camille about what they saw when they came in that morning. Neither were willing to leave their wounded dogs' side until the shelter's volunteer vets got there to care for them.

Within minutes of each other, Dr. Izzy and Dr. Dylan arrived at the shelter. Both had abandoned their private practices for the day and came flying into the adoption-side dog run to tend to their most important patients. Camille heard Dr. Izzy before she saw her. Her voice was shrill as she explained to a cop standing guard outside the building who she was and why she needed to be allowed inside. Her shoes smacked along the tile floor after he let her through and she ran past Willa and Hollywood, who were being taken care of by Dr. Dylan, and came straight to Caleb.

"Oh my god," she breathed when she saw the athletic pitbull lying on his side next to Camille. His little tippy tail wag brushed against the cold floor and the fear and rage in her eyes was replaced with care and tenderness as she moved in closer to gauge his condition.

"How's he doing?" Dr. Dylan yelled over to Dr. Izzy. His voice bounced off the walls in the uncharacteristically quiet dog run. All the condos were occupied, which meant 20 dogs were silent while they watched cops mill around their shelter and two well-known vets take care of their fellow housemates. It was an eerie, yet amazing sight.

Dr. Izzy replied, "He's lost a tooth from a head wound, has a sprained, possible broken front paw, a small cut on his back and a probable concussion. He needs a CT scan to look for bleeding in the brain, an x-ray of this leg, and a full work up. I can take him back to my office in case he needs surgery, but he'll definitely need 24-hour care for a while. How about you?"

"Hollywood definitely needs stitches for this large laceration on his thigh. It's almost 8 inches in length and he might need a transfusion since he lost so much blood. You have that capability at your office, right?"

Dr. Izzy ran a state-of-the-art surgical veterinary practice with all the latest and greatest equipment, while Dr. Dylan's practice focused more on everyday care and annual exams. He had a small surgical area but nothing like Dr. Izzy and he referred a lot of his clients who needed more complex procedures to her.

"Yeah, and one of my veterinary nurses is on her way here with our mobile care van, so we can load them both in there and get started on them while we head back to my office. Anything else going on with Mr. Hollywood?" she asked while she checked Caleb's vitals again.

"Yeah, he has a gash on his head and ear, which might need stitches, but I'd suggest a CT scan for him too to check for bleeding. How far out is she?"

"I'm here!" came a voice from the lobby. "I'm here!"

Seconds later, a young woman in her late-20's dashed into the room carrying two fold-up stretchers under each arm. She was breathing heavy but never slowed down and the graphic sights before her didn't seem to register, as she tried to stay in work mode.

"Cierra, over here!" yelled Dr. Izzy.

A cop grabbed one of the stretchers from Cierra and took it to Dr. Dylan and Hollywood while Cierra brought the other to Dr. Izzy and Caleb.

"Holy hell, Dr. Iz," she said as she unfolded the stretcher and moved to help place Caleb onto it. "Holy hell."

"I know, I know. Deep breaths, everyone. Let's get these two back to my office pronto!" She coached as the significance of the situation enveloped everyone.

The vets had Willa and Camille help maneuver their prospective dogs onto their stretchers and quickly got them out to the mobile veterinary van. They then sped off, with a police escort, to Dr. Izzy's practice and left Willa and Camille behind.

They gave more detailed statements to the detectives in charge and got a better look at all the damage done to their beloved shelter. Thousands of dollars of destruction covered the walls, floors, and ceilings of the building. All the dog and cat food in the "food shed" had been cut open and sprayed down with some liquid chemical, possibly an insect killer spray they kept around for bug control. The laundry area was ransacked and flooded. Many of the windows were broken and the fence outside was knocked down and spray-painted.

Steve's office was one of the hardest hit areas, with his computer, desk, filing cabinets, and basically everything in there, ruined. The only clue as to why someone would do this to the Ocean Pals Shelter Animal was found in his office. A message spray-painted along his wall, which read, "There will be more. $$$ or else."

Chapter 11

SAILOR & JC

"I hate to say this, but your club is in serious trouble. You need to drastically cut your expenses, increase your prices, and possibly lease out some space to other tenants. Have you ever thought about renting out for conferences, weddings, or parties? That could be a good—"

JC cut Trevor off mid-sentence, "Oh, no, big guy. X-nay on the wedding talk, eh? I don't do stuff like that. My club is for my parties only."

Trevor tapped his fingers against the mahogany bar and pondered how to say this delicately. Unable to find the words, he went for brazen instead.

"If you don't rent out for conferences or weddings, then you'll be closed and putting up a giant for sale sign instead. Is that better?"

JC allowed the words sink in and slumped onto one of the cheetah-print upholstered stools that lined the bar.

"Ughhh, no, Trevor. No." He huffed as he dropped his head into his hands. "I just . . . didn't think it had gotten this bad. I thought maybe I was overlooking something. And I, sure as shit, don't want to be a party planner!"

Trevor could see that JC was finally starting to take his financial situation more seriously, but he felt bad for the guy, especially since he knew how crappy it was to be in a monetary mess like him.

"Look, man, I know it's not ideal, but you don't have to *be* the party planner. You can hire one or . . . a better financial solution would be for you to put it out there that you're looking to take on a business partner who can handle the party planning portion of your business."

"What do you mean . . . business partner?" JC squinted at Trevor, his hesitation and confusion apparent.

"Well, you can structure it however you'd like but the typical partnership goes like this: You offer 30% of your stake in the company to your business partner and they pay you a lump sum upfront to buy into the business. Then, from there on out, profits are split 70/30 and you dictate the terms on who handles what up front in a formal contract.

You can stipulate that the contract is re-negotiated every year, three years, or whatever you feel comfortable with, but it's a win-win for both parties. You'll get an influx of cash and they'll get a portion of the business."

JC stared at Trevor as the wheels in his brain turned and he tried to understand this new business idea.

"I don't know. I mean, it sounds great in theory but even though I'm a team player, I don't know how I feel about someone getting their grubby little hands on *MY* business."

"It's something you need to consider. Think about it, talk it over with Ryan, and let me know if you have any questions. But look at it this way bro, you need a bigger band-aid than what you have available here to stop the money from hemorrhaging. If things stay the way they are, your business will be a lost cause by next quarter and there will be no going back. Try not to think with your emotions on this, use your business sense and the hard facts. Be analytical."

"Right, sure, that wonderful business sense that got me into this mess in the first place. Is there any way I could sink some more of my own cash into the business to keep it afloat? I have a nice chunk still saved from my baseball days . . .

Although, it's a chunk we kind of had allotted for something else."

Trevor read between the lines and nodded, "Sure, you could do that but if you don't change the business plan from what it is now, you'll be in the same position in another year or two. Just . . . from one guy, trying to get by, to another, don't cut off your nose to spite your face."

JC's forehead crinkled as he looked at Trevor like he had six heads.

"Don't what?"

"Cut off your nose to spite your face? Shoot yourself in the foot, don't overreact to this situation in a way that will negatively affect other parts of your life."

JC continued to stare at Trevor, his bewilderment splashed across his tan face.

"Dude, don't screw up your home life to make this money pit work. That's what your club is right now . . . a money pit. You need more diversity in your profits. You need new ways to make money. Just throwing parties during the summer isn't cutting it with all the new bars and clubs popping up around the area. You need more and you have the unique opportunity to rebrand your club and offer new and exciting options for people looking to host their functions in Ocean Park."

JC's eyes closed slowly at the realization that things at Spinners had to change. He had to adapt or die.

"Fine. I hear you. I'll talk it over with Ryan and will let you know if we want to put word out there that I'm looking for a partner. You can help with that, right?"

"Yeah, I can help find someone and facilitate the financial aspects of the deal, but I strongly suggest that you have a lawyer involved too."

"I can do that. Camille is my lawyer."

"Camille from the shelter?" Trevor asked.

"Yeah, you remember her from when you adopted this pretty girl, right?"

JC reached down to pet Athena, who lounged at their feet on the cold, concrete floor. JC had offered her a dog bed that he used to keep in his office when his old dog, Molly, had been alive. She had come to work with him every day and he couldn't bear to move her bed after she passed away, so it stayed where he could see it and remember her.

Athena wanted nothing to do with the bed and proudly lay on the floor, with her body plastered up against Trevor's feet. Talk about a daddy's girl.

"Oh yeah, absolutely. She and Sammi were cool."

JC spotted an opening when Trevor stumbled over Sammi's name.

"Hell yeah, they are. So, I couldn't help but notice you and Sammi had, sort of, a connection, right?"

Playing matchmaker was JC's second favorite game to play.

His suspicions were proven right when Trevor blushed and dropped his head forward a little before he rubbed his hand over the back of his neck while he answered, "Uh, yeah, I guess you could say that. Do you know if she's seeing anyone?"

"Oh my god, no. That girl is more available than anyone in the history of the universe. She did just get out of a 10-year relationship awhile back, but she's awesome and you'd be lucky to date her. You want her number?"

JC doesn't mess around when it comes to matchmaking.

"Yeah, please. That'd be great. I just got out of a long-term relationship a year ago too, so we have that in common."

JC reached across the bar for his phone as he replied back to Trevor, "Yeah, maybe don't lead with that on your first date."

Trevor laughed and then groaned as he thought about going on his first date since his divorce. He watched as JC unlocked his phone and his face went white.

"Whoa, what's wrong? You okay?"

"Willa texted me. There was a break-in at the shelter last night. A few dogs were hurt and the place was trashed. Sweet Jesus, I gotta go."

"What? Holy shit, man."

"Yeah, I don't know but I gotta get over there. They need help relocating the dogs and cats. Sorry to cut this short, but—"

"No, no worries. Let's go. I can help too."

JC stopped for a second and looked Trevor up and down in surprise.

"Freakin' Sammi, gettin' the hunky animal-loving sexpot. Not fair, man, not fair at all."

JC and Trevor raced over to Ocean Pals, breaking numerous laws on the way there. Speeding, failure to stop at stop signs, and tailgating were just to name a few.

Since it was a cold, December day, Trevor was able to leave Athena in his truck while they went inside and helped handle things at the shelter.

JC spotted Willa first and ran over to her, "Willa, what happened? Is everyone okay?"

A stoic Willa turned to JC and started to explain, but he pulled her into a giant hug first and squeezed her tight. After a few seconds, she pulled away but thanked him for the hug she didn't know she needed.

"Basically, someone broke in and trashed the place. Hollywood and Caleb must have broken out of their kennels because they were the only ones hurt and both their cages look smashed from the inside. I guess their protective nature took over and they reacted as if someone was breaking into their home. They both have serious injuries, but we did just hear back from the vets and they're expected to fully recover. It'll just take time and lots of love."

"Are there any leads on who it might've been?" Trevor chimed in and Willa shook her head at him.

"Not at the moment, at least not that I know of. The cops left a while ago and said they'd be in touch. They want to talk to Steve, but no one can get a hold of him. They were going to stop by his house, I think, on their way back to the station."

JC looked around the chaotic shelter in disbelief. Who would do this to his beautiful babies? Who would attack an animal shelter? How awful of a human being do you have to be to want to hurt homeless animals and the people who help them?

He squeezed his eyes shut tight and balled his fists in anger.

"What the fuck?" he exploded. "Who in the hell has to be so messed up that they would come in here and do this to our shelter? What is wrong with people?" His arms gestured wildly, and his voice grew louder and louder, with everyone turning to look his way.

"We already deal with such shitty situations when people want to discard their pets like trash or when they let them loose and we bring them here after they've been found hit by a car. Why did someone have to take it a step further and do this?"

He yelled as he pointed to the walls where graffiti covered the shiny, egg white paint.

"Or this?" he angrily pointed to the reception desk, ruined beyond repair.

"Or fucking this?" His voice broke as he pointed towards the dog's condo area where Hollywood and Caleb were attacked.

"They hurt our babies."

The words came out with a growl as his emotions bubbled out of control.

Camille appeared out of the crowd, wrapped her arms around JC, and he collapsed into her embrace. Tears flowed from their eyes as Willa joined them for a group hug. One by one, the other volunteers piled on until everyone was hugging and mourning the violent, unthinkable act done to their shelter and their furbabies.

Slowly, the 15 or so people tightly wrapped around each other started to pull away and drifted back to work. JC held Willa and Camille tight for a final few seconds before speaking, "I'm sorry ladies. I just . . ."

"Don't be sorry. We get it. We're pissed too. We've had more time to process this than you. We've gone through the five stages of grief a few times already. You still have a few more laps to go."

Camille's words made JC laugh and a smile finally reached his face.

"I just can't believe it," he said.

Tough as nails Willa chimed in, "Well, believe it because it happened and now, we need to deal with it. We started to come up with a plan since Steve isn't here."

"What have you got so far?" JC asked, noticing that she was ready to get to the point and get back to work.

"We need to find temporary foster homes for all the animals, so we can get this place cleaned up and back in business."

"I'll send out an urgent email and text to all our current volunteers," JC said, since he had a file with everyone's contact info.

Camille spoke up, "I'll reach out to a few of my media contacts to see if they can get us on the local news tonight. Maybe we can get some extra foster homes that way?"

"Good idea," Willa said, "You guys run with those tasks and Trevor and I will go out back and try to fix the fence so we can get some of these dogs out to pee."

She turned to get to work before she spun back around and yelled out to the group, "Good job everyone. Thank you for your help. Let's keep on working. The animals need us!"

"Babe, you would not believe the day I had," JC called out to Ryan as he walked through the front door of their large colonial style home with a surprise in tow.

Ryan came down the hallway, from the kitchen to the foyer, to meet JC for his welcome home kiss but stopped short when he saw Sailor.

"Who is this?" he asked as he leaned down to let her sniff his hand.

"This is Sailor. I'm hoping she can stay with us for a while." JC said sweetly, trying to skip over the part where he didn't mention he was bringing a foster dog home when he texted earlier.

Ryan stroked Sailor's head as she looked up at him with her bright, yellow eyes. "She's beautiful. Why is she staying with us?"

Sailor jumped up and put her paws on Ryan's chest and stretched out her tiny body to give him a soft kiss on his chin. Ryan returned the gesture and scratched her belly as she closed her beautiful eyes in bliss. JC didn't answer and let Sailor work her magic on Ryan, hoping she'd charm him just like she did to JC.

Sailor was a hyper girl who needed a home with a family who would run with her and throw the ball all day long. She needed a job to do to keep her out of trouble and exercise was the perfect job for her. Once she was tired out, her 25-pound body could finally relax and she turned into a little brindle cuddle bug that would wrap up next to you on the couch and share your popcorn.

She was overlooked at the shelter by most adopters because she barked at people when they passed by her condo and her bark was quite high-pitched and came off a little aggressively shrill. At 2-years old, she'd been at Ocean Pals for over six months and spent another six months at a rural shelter in western Maryland. The girl was more than ready to find her forever home and as sweet as she was, JC was always surprised the right family hadn't come for her yet.

Ryan didn't press for an answer and instead, he stood up quickly and declared, "Wait, just tell me all about it over dinner. I'm starving and haven't eaten a thing all day."

JC followed his husband to the kitchen, "But you . . . feed people all day from the food truck? You're surrounded by food. How can you not eat?"

Ryan chuckled a soft laugh and rolled his eyes, "Yeah, I know. You would think, but I just didn't have any time. We were slammed from the moment we opened to the moment we closed. Since it's just me handling the prep and cooking, while Candi takes the orders, there's no time for breaks."

JC watched as his exhausted husband sat down at the table and poured them each a glass of wine. He was filled with immense pride and gratitude for the man in front of him. Sailor, with her leash still attached in case they need to quickly grab her, followed them both into the kitchen and sat down next to them at the table, like she'd always been a part of their group.

"You're amazing, babe. You really need to think about opening your own restaurant soon. At least, then, one of us could be a successful business owner."

Ryan picked up on JC's self-deprecation, "The restaurant can wait. How did that meeting go today?"

JC groaned and took a long gulp of his wine before he answered, "Not great. Trevor said I need to sell, become a party planner, or bring on a business partner who can put on weddings and events since the whole bar/dance club idea isn't working."

"How do you feel about that?"

"Terrible. But what choice do I have? We need to talk it over more, but I think it's the way things have to be if I want to keep the club."

"I'm sorry, JC. I know that's not what you want."

"Yeah, well, that wasn't even the worst part of my day."

After another long gulp of wine, which resulted in him finishing his glass, JC poured another hefty dose of vino and told Ryan about the break-in at the shelter and why they were fostering Sailor.

Always the good sport, Ryan embraced their new role as temporary foster pawrents to Sailor. The two men cleaned up the kitchen and were finishing up the dishes when JC remembered something he wanted to ask Ryan.

"Ry, why did you say earlier that the restaurant would have to wait? Isn't that what you've always wanted?"

Ryan slowly closed the dishwasher and turned to JC, a look of insecurity across his face.

"Yeah, I still do want to have my own restaurant someday, but . . . but I want to wait until you have the club and its finances under control and . . ."

He stopped short and bit at his lower lip while he rubbed his fingers together, his telltale sign that he was nervous.

JC stepped towards him, took one of his hands and squeezed it into his own, and waited until Ryan made eye contact with him to speak up, "What is it? You can tell me anything."

"I'm ready for us to adopt. I want us to have a kid before we open a restaurant."

JC felt an elephant land on his chest as he tried not to outwardly react to Ryan's declaration. Yeah, he wanted a family, but now? Right now?

So, he asked, "Ready like . . . you're ready now?"

"Yep. I'd like to start the foster-to-adopt classes next month."

Gulp.

Chapter 12
ZIGGY and Sammi

"Ladies, you only have 15-minutes left on this event until we move over to beam. Start trying to wrap up your five first halves and five second halves now." Sammi yelled out to her gymnasts who were practicing on bars.

It was 1:30pm and she'd already been at the gym for six hours and still had another two hours to go. Typically, she coached at night but since the kids were off school for winter break, they had moved all the team practices to the daytime, so the gym wasn't so cramped. It allowed the girls to be there longer and get in some extra hours before their competition season ramped up after the holidays.

"Don't forget your dismounts are included in the second half of your routine. If you need to, you can do two into the pit onto an 8-incher before doing the last three onto a competition landing."

She saw a few eye rolls at this last comment but let it go without saying anything. She remembered being a teenage gymnast and how some days, everything your coach said or did could cause an eye roll. Plus, these girls put their bodies through hell doing this sport. Many of them had constant aches and pains and some had mental blocks and were terrified of their skills. They were tough, strong young women who pushed through fear and pain for a sport they all loved dearly. So, that was why she let their attitudes go some days. Well, that, and because it would be a constant battle if she didn't.

The gymnasts bounced from one set of bars to another and back to the chalk bucket, where they filled their leather grips with white powder to help them hold onto the bars better. They all had their own way of putting chalk onto their grips and some were more specific about it than others. A few swipes of the chalk block, then a spray of water from a small squirt bottle, rub your grips together, then add some loose chalk to your grips again, and finish with a dab of your own spit and you're good to go. At least, that was Sammi's routine when she was a gymnast many moons ago.

She felt her phone vibrate in her pocket as she watched Mya, a 17-year-old level 10 gymnast, perform the first half of her bar routine. The girls' assignment for the day was to complete five first halves of their routines and five second halves, so Mya started her routine standing in the between the bars with her back facing the high bar and she jumped to kip onto the low bar. She glided through and hit a strong handstand and then dropped her body down into a free hip circle around the bar and threw herself up towards the high bar in a Shaposhnikova, a skill named for the first gymnast who ever performed it in international competition, Natalia Shaposhnikova. Mya finished up the first half of her routine with another tight cast to handstand into a Tkatchev, where she launched her body over the high bar in a straddle position and then re-caught the bar. Then, after that, she swung down into her Pak salto release to the low bar. She hopped down from another hit handstand and yelled out to Sammi, "That was my fifth first half."

The gym was a loud place with music playing, equipment being moved, and a lot of people talking, so Sammi had to call out back over to her, "Good job. You hit a better position in the Shaposh that time. Did you feel it?"

"Yeah, I could tell and my overshoot felt better too. Second halves now?"

"Yup. Good job." Sammi answered.

This went on for another few hours until she and the girls were all exhausted and ready to head home for the day.

"Awesome job today, ladies. You're all doing really well, but we have some more hard work coming our way next week. Rest up this weekend and I'll see you on Monday!"

The gymnasts all filed out of the practice gym and headed home as Sammi and the other coaches cleaned up the gym before they left. Sammi didn't get to check her phone until just after 3:45pm when she was walking to her car.

Her heart all but stopped when she saw the words on her phone screen from Camille. She had texts and emails from Willa, JC, and another unknown number too, but she skipped past them and focused on Camille's message.

She re-read it and then broke into a sprint to her car. She made the 20-minute drive home in record time and ran into the house to see if her mom, Ruth, had any more details about what happened, but she was nowhere to be found.

"Mom?" Sammi yelled. "Where are you? I just heard about what happened at the shelter and . . . Jesus, Mom? Where in the hell?"

Her words trailed off when she spotted her mom through a window in the kitchen outside in her garden. She turned and pulled open the back door and stalked out across the backyard yelling to her mom, who still didn't hear her.

"Mom!" Sammi yelled and waved her arms wildly in front of her mother, who was clipping dead leaves off her kale plants.

Ruth finally saw her daughter and jumped about a foot off the ground. She brought her hand to her heart and checked to see if it was still beating.

"Holy hell, you scared me!" she cried.

"Mom, I've been calling your name since I got home a few minutes ago. What are you doing out here anyways? It's freezing and that kale looks dead."

"Well, you know I've been bored since I broke my hip so I wanted to see if I could revive my garden and well . . . it looks like I can't, but that's not the point—"

Sammi couldn't take it anymore and interrupted, "Did you hear about the break-in at the shelter?"

Ruth looked at her like she was an alien asking her for her hand in marriage.

"What?" she asked, her voice reaching an almost jarring level.

"I got a text from everyone. Emails too. Did you get any? Where's your phone?"

Ruth patted her jacket pockets, then her pants pockets, and then started to trudge into the house to look for her misplaced phone.

"Moooom," Sammi groaned. "Why do you have a phone if you never keep it with you? What if you fall again?"

"Oh, would you stop. First off, that was a fluke thing and you know I hate that damn phone." She retraced her steps through the house and located her lost phone, which had 10 missed calls and many more texts.

"Geez, Ms. Popular, how long has it been since you last checked that thing? Like days?"

Ruth gave her daughter a discouraged look and scrolled through the messages.

"What happened? Tell me what you know," she demanded.

"Just that there was a break-in and they need some temporary foster homes."

"Let's go, you're driving." Ruth jumped to action and Sammi followed closely behind.

On the drive there, Ruth connected with her friends and fellow volunteers at the shelter and got the whole story, which she relayed to Sammi.

"Okay, they said Gracie, Ziggy, Seely, and Destiny still need foster homes, plus two cats who both need to be the only felines in the home. Who should we take? I don't know most of them anymore since I've been off with my hip, so it's your call. Who would work best for us?"

"Aww, Ziggy. Let's bring that snuggly boy home. He'll keep you company while I'm at work. He's low maintenance and you know him since he's been there a long time now. What has it been? Almost a year, maybe?"

"Yeah, I do love that sweet boy. He's big but he hates walks . . . or at least he did when I was there . . . that still true?" Ruth asked Sammi.

"Oh yeah, big time. He's still happy to just lay in the yard, snuggle on the couch, or do anything that involves relaxing. How old is he?"

Ruth thought to herself for a few seconds before she replied, "I think he's 6 or 7. He's such a low-key guy until another dog walks by his condo, then he goes ape shit. But I think that's just his way of communicating and wanting to play."

Sammi nodded, "I agree and I think it scares a lot of people when they hear him bark. He's a 60-pound chow-mix who has this big voice, but if they got to know him a bit, they'd see that he's a sweetie pie underneath all that soft, caramel-y brindle fur. The shelter environment is stressful enough for these dogs and people come in and expect them to be well-behaved, but it's still a place where they're confined with lots of other animals with lots of smells and random people walking around. But when Ziggy is out of his condo, he doesn't want anything to do with the other dogs. He just wants attention from people and to get lots of pets and give lots of kisses."

Ruth and Sammi pulled up to the shelter and headed inside to see the damage and to offer to open up their home as a temporary foster for Ziggy. They were in and out in less than 30-minutes and Ziggy rode home with his head out the opened window the whole way.

"Seriously, that was the coldest ride home ever," Sammi said as she shivered when they were finally home and were settled in. "But seeing his happy face made it worth it."

Ruth handed her a cup of hot tea and sat down on the opposite end of the couch. Ziggy jumped up in between them and made himself at home. He placed his head on Ruth's feet as she scratched his ears and his tail slapped up and down against Sammi's lap as she scrolled through her phone.

A huge smile spread across her face as she read a text. She set her hot mug down on the brown table next to their blue couch to give it her full attention.

Ruth eyed her curiously and finally the suspense got to be too much, "What is it?" she asked, smiling herself since Sammi's grin had a way of being infectious.

"Do you remember that guy, Trevor, I told you about from the shelter? The one who adopted Athena?" her eyes shined as she recounted the story to her mom.

"Yeah, the hot, sexpot accountant, right?"

Her mom was never one to hold back or filter her words.

"Yeah. He texted me earlier and asked me out for coffee this weekend."

Sammi's eyes moved from her phone to meet her mom's in a flash and they both had wildly different reactions.

While at first it seemed like Sammi was excited, her reaction flip-flopped to dread. She buried her head in her hands and groaned while Ruth threw her hands into the air and did a little happy dance. All this excitement got Ziggy going and he joined in with a few woofs of his own.

"See Ziggy thinks you should go out with him! He just said so," Ruth laughed, but her daughter looked sick with anxiety. Her voice softened, "Sweetie, you need to date again at some point. You won't be alone forever, so why not get back out there with a hot guy who obviously loves dogs like you do? You never know, it may be a dud of a date but it might go really well too."

Sammi groaned again, "I know, I know, but just thinking about getting ready, going out on a date, and putting myself out there again really makes me want to crawl into a hole and never come out again." She slapped her hands over her face and moaned again, "I haaaaaate first dates. They're so weird and uncomfortable and we both always act so fake and put on this dumb show—"

Ruth interrupted her daughter's whine fest, "And if you don't go on the first date, then you never make it to a second or third or, eventually, happily ever after. So, do yourself a favor and go be uncomfortable for a night. Put yourself out there. You said he was hot, hot, hot and you couldn't stop talking about him for a while. Don't let your fear stand in your way. Don't you say that to your gymnasts from time to time?"

Sammi gave her mom the stink eye and took a few seconds before she replied, "Yes, and fine. Fine, I'll go, but I'm going to complain a lot about it, so just . . . you're going to have to deal with it."

"I can handle that," Ruth said as she grinned at her daughter.

She knew Sammi put up a tough front and was terrified of getting hurt again. That's why she pushed her to say yes to this guy and get out there on a first date. She had two dates since her breakup and she acted this way before both of those too. Unfortunately, those two turned out to be super duds so Ruth said a quick plea to the universe, *Please let the third time be the charm*.

"Huh?" Sammi asked, pulling her head up from her phone where she was typing away.

"Oh, nothing," Ruth lied, realizing she must have said the words out loud instead of just in her head. "Did you get back to him?"

"Yeah, we're going out tomorrow afternoon. 1pm at Macklin's Coffee. God, I'm a nervous wreck already." She held her hand out so Ruth could see that it was shaking.

"It'll be fine, sweetie. It'll be fine."

Sammi's phone dinged again and so did Ruth's from its spot under Ziggy's big head.

Sammi clicked hers open as Ruth tried to slide her hand under the dog's heavy noggin. He wasn't helping her out at all by lifting his head or moving it off to the side, in fact, it seemed like he was pushing it down harder against the couch, so she couldn't get to her phone.

"Buddy, I promise I'll keep petting you if you let me have my phone. I'm not on it all the time like

137

this one over here," she told the dog as she gestured to Sammi.

She leaned her head down toward him as she dug around for her phone and he quickly lifted up and layered a few coats of dog slobber on her face in the form of kisses. At least she was able to get to her phone.

"Seriously?" Sammi said in shock.

Ruth swiped her phone open and read the text that had come in and resonated a similar response.

"Holy crap," she said. "They still can't find him?"

Before Sammi could answer, her phone rang and she picked up right away.

"JC, what's going on?" she asked, her voice full of question and concern.

"No one can find him. The police went to his house and his wife hasn't seen him since the morning before the attack. We have to wait until morning to file an official police report, but the detectives working on the shelter break-in are still looking for him since he's a person of interest in their case."

"Do you think he was still there during the break-in? Does he stay late sometimes?" Sammi asked, since JC had volunteered there a lot longer than her.

"Not usually that late, but who knows. Hopefully he's okay, but we can't get a hold of Emily either and it's just really strange that they're both out of commission at a time like this."

"Yeah, strange. And sort of suspicious."

"Ain't that the truth, girl." JC agreed.

Chapter 13

SEELY and Camille

Camille pulled her car up to her ranch home, turned off the engine, and released her head back to hit the headrest with a deep sigh. To say that today had been a long day was a complete understatement. She was only supposed to be at the shelter from 8 a.m. until 11 a.m., but ended up staying until almost 10 that evening because of the break-in. It was one of the longest days of her life, not counting Damien's birth which lasted for almost 40 hours.

Speaking of Damien, she was dreading the conversation they had to have tonight.

She had already called and filled Max in on what happened since he was expecting her home before lunch. He offered to come help, but she didn't want Damien anywhere near the disaster at the shelter. She knew he would be devastated to hear about Caleb's injuries and his serious condition.

She pulled herself from the car with a grunt and headed inside. As she opened the front door, sounds of video games playing in the living room greeted her. Max paused the game as soon as he saw her and got up to envelope her in a big hug. She melted into his arms and fought back tears. She didn't want to cry in front of Damien, but she wasn't sure if she could help it. Between her exhaustion and heavy turmoil from the day, she didn't have much control over her emotions anymore.

She pulled away from Max and then stood on her tiptoes to give him a kiss. Their lips lingered for a few seconds before they pulled away and looked towards Damien.

"Can you turn that game off and come sit with me?" she asked him.

He eyed her wearily, sensing something was amiss with his mom. He turned the game off and moved from his place on the floor to sit next to her on their gray couch.

"Damien, there was a break-in at the shelter last night. Some bad people came in and tore the place apart. That's why I was there so long today."

He looked at her, his eyes serious and concerned.

"Is everybody okay? Is Caleb okay?" the words tumbled out of his mouth, like he couldn't control them.

She felt her lips pinch together as she took a second to word her response correctly. He looked like a young child again as he stared at her, waiting for her reply. She'd been so worried about him growing up and not needing her anymore that she forgot he still does. He does need her, just in a new and different way. She'd always be his mom and he'd always look to her for guidance.

"He's going to be okay, but he has a long road ahead of him. He's at a vet hospital and they're taking very good care of him—"

He interrupted, "Can we visit him? Mom, what happened? Why would someone hurt him?"

She grabbed his hand and gave it a squeeze.

"We don't know why yet, sweetie, but we're going to find out. And I think he'd love for us to come visit once he's feeling better. Maybe in a few weeks."

"Well, I'd like to go as soon as we can. I'm the reason he's there in the first place. It's my fault and—"

Now it was her turn to cut him off, "No. Damien, it is *not* your fault. Absolutely not."

"But—"

"No buts. No nothing. It is not your fault. You helped him that day in the park and when he finds his forever home, he'll have you to thank for that."

After a long sigh, he looked to his dad and said, "For Christmas, I want all the money you'd spend on presents, to go to the shelter."

"Bud, we already bought all your gifts," Max said gently from his spot on the opposite couch.

"Take them back. I don't want to celebrate Christmas while Caleb is hurt. I don't understand why anyone would do this in the first place."

He stood up and stalked down the hallway to his room but turned and said one last thing before he slammed the door, "I want to go see Caleb and I want to go tomorrow. With or without you."

The shock she was feeling from Damien's reaction was too much for her tired body to handle and Camille just shrugged at Max.

"I don't think I can argue with him about that."

"We'll handle it in the morning. Let's go to bed and see how we're all feeling tomorrow."

Camille nodded and took Max's outstretched hand to help her stand. They walked entwined together to their bedroom where Camille skipped her nighttime routine and fell into bed, fully clothed. She kicked off her pants, bra, and long thermal and fell asleep almost immediately.

The next morning, the smell of coffee welcomed her awake and she threw on some sweats and headed to the kitchen. Damien and Max were eating breakfast and Duke was lounging at their feet. The 100-pound mutt rolled over to greet her, showed his stomach and wagged his tail from his upside-down position. She gave his belly a few scratches before she poured herself a cup of much needed coffee and sat down at the table with her guys.

"Morning," she mumbled.

"When can we go see Caleb?" Damien asked immediately.

With a sigh she replied, "I don't know that we can, sweetie."

"Well, can you ask?"

Not looking for a fight this early in the morning, she gave in and replied with a slight eye roll, so he knew she wasn't happy about it, "Sure."

He stared at her.

"What?"

"Like . . . now? Can you ask now?"

"Damien, give your mom a chance to wake up before you start demanding things from her," Max's stern voice chimed in.

Damien huffed and got up from the table. He headed back to his room with Duke on his heels. The door slammed *again* and Camille's shoulders jumped to her ears from the noise.

"Welcome to the teenage years," Max said as he rubbed his temples.

A grunt passed through Camille's lips. Still drained from the last 24-hours, she had no other response left in her. Max started to clean up their breakfast dishes and Camille wrapped her arms in front of her and put her head down on the table for a few more minutes of rest.

Her phone beeped, ignoring her peace, and she groaned when it beeped again and again.

"What?" she barked at it as she turned to look at its stupid, tiny screen.

She read the messages twice before looking at Max. He noticed her funny expression and asked with caution, "What?"

"That was JC. He's in charge of finding foster homes for all the dogs. They still need a home for Seely."

She raised her eyebrows to Max and he seemed to sense where this conversation was about to go.

"Babe, I don't know what you're thinking. Well, I do think I know what you're thinking, but I don't know that we can take on a foster dog right now. Look how attached Damien got to this Caleb and he never even lived here."

"I know, I know, but maybe this would be a good thing for him. He needs to learn that he can't bring home every single dog he helps. If we temporarily foster Seely, it would be a good life lesson for Damien. To have to go through a little pain in order to do something good for someone else."

Max shook his head and said, "Yeah, okay, sure, but what about Duke? You know he's not super fond of other dogs. What if they don't get along?"

"We'll figure it out. We'll supervise them at all times and I don't think we give Duke enough credit. I think our fear of him and other dogs really overshadows his true actions."

"I don't think it's a good idea."

"Well, if he just happens to be here tonight? Would you be mad?"

"Camille . . ."

"Just come to the shelter with me today and meet him. They need help with more clean up anyways and since you're on break, maybe you could stop by for a few hours? Damien too."

Max gave in, "Fine. But you better find out if Damien can see Caleb or not before we get him involved too."

Camille groaned and then called out to her husband, who was on his way to their bedroom, "Thank you, hun. You're the best!"

She got a halfhearted, "Yeah, whatever" with a hand wave, as he kept moving towards their room.

Camille finished her coffee and hopped up to get ready, suddenly feeling more energized than she did a few minutes ago. She had a good feeling about today. She wasn't sure why, but something clicked and her mood went from dog-tired and pessimistic to excited and hopeful.

"Hey, Willa," Camille called out as she walked into the shelter a few hours later. Max and Damien were coming by in an hour after Damien's indoor soccer practice, but Willa had asked Camille to come in early.

Willa walked out of Steve's still-trashed office. "Hey, can I get your opinion on something quick?"

"Sure."

"Can you look over these documents and tell me what you think they mean?"

She handed a folder to Camille.

"I'm trying to sort out all this stuff in Steve's office since he's still not back. The Board asked me to go over the finances and they want a full audit of all the documents, shelter procedures, and well, basically, everything. And they asked me to do it."

She looked frazzled at the overwhelming task.

"It makes sense," Camille said as she peeked into Steve's disaster zone of an office. "The break-in probably has them worried and they just want to cover their asses. Let me know if you need any help. Have you ever done an audit before?"

"Yeah, I worked for my parent's financial company before I had kids. I did audits like this all the time, but it's been over 20 years so I'm a little rusty. Plus, a lot of these documents don't make much sense. I'm sure I'll be here all night."

Camille patted her friend on the back and gave her a sympathetic look, "I'm sorry. I'll pitch in anywhere I can. What can I do now?"

"Just look those over and then . . . foster Seely. That would be wonderful," a laugh escaped her lips, along with a wink as she said it.

"Oh, that's all huh?" Camille joked back.

The two laughed at their silly interaction and then looked at all the paper strewn around the room. This made them laugh harder and the two fell into a fit from sheer exhaustion.

The front door opened and Max and Damien walked in to find the two women on the floor, gasping for breath as they continued their laugh-a-thon.

"What's so funny?" Damien asked as he and his dad looked at the two ladies like they'd lost it.

This made them laugh harder and it was a few moments before they could keep their cool long enough to answer.

"I have no idea," Camille giggled as she and Willa worked their way off the floor.

"Yeah, I don't know what got us going, but I guess we needed it," Willa said with a smile spread across her face.

"You guys are weird," Damien said before he walked away to check out the rest of the shelter.

Camille and Willa shrugged at each other before Camille asked Max why they were there so early.

"I forgot Damien's soccer practice was cancelled this week because the gym is closed for the holidays. So, we came over here to help out."

"And to see Seely?" Camille asked.

"Well, I was sort of hoping you had forgotten about that part but, yeah, I guess," Max replied.

"He's on the recovery side. Those kennels weren't damaged as much and need minimal repairs." Willa said as she dove back into her paperwork.

Camille led Max over to the recovery side and as soon as he saw Seely, he busted into laughter.

"Oh my god, Camille. He's about as wide as he is tall."

Camille opened his condo and carried the 30-pound dog back to the fenced area for them to formally meet. When Seely's paws hit the ground, he waddled over to Max and his little tail wiggled back and forth with every step.

She watched Max melt and fall in love in front of her. He smiled at the little guy who needed to lose a good 10 to 15 pounds. His wiry fur was a cream color and his round belly dragged on the ground as his little legs moved him forward. His rotund body dwarfed his tiny face, but his eyes were kind and soulful.

Max knelt down to meet the big, little guy as Damien came out of the building to find them.

His eyes lit up as he ran over to meet Seely.

"What's his name?" he asked.

"Seely. He needs a foster home," Max said as Damien got covered in welcoming kisses from the young pup.

"Can we take him?" he asked, excitement rippling through his words.

Max looked up at Camille and gave her a little smirk, knowing this was her plan all along. She knew Seely would win them over and make it impossible for him to say no.

"Yeah, but just temporarily," Max emphasized. "And only if Duke likes him too."

Damien jumped up and ran around the play area as Seely followed him, barking and jumping up at his feet.

"You're going to have to help walk him, Damien," Max called out to him.

Camille wrapped her arms around her husband as they watched their son and new foster dog run laps around the yard, "Maybe this'll be good for all of us."

Chapter 14

SAILOR and JC

"What do I do?" JC asked Willa as they sipped on wine and went over more of the complicated documents from Steve's office.

JC had called Willa after his discussion with Ryan about adoption and they agreed to meet up the next evening. When Willa was still working on going over the shelter's financial documents for her upcoming audit, she invited him there so she didn't have to cancel completely.

They sat on the floor surrounded by a moat of stark white computer paper dribbled with impossible, illogical letters and numbers. Their wine helped make it all better.

"What do you want to do?" she asked, grateful to not be staring at puzzling numbers for a while.

"I want to adopt, but just not yet. I don't know if we're ready now. I mean, my club is on life support and I thought we'd have more money and time and have everything figured out before we started the process. I don't feel like we're ready."

"Well, first off, you never feel completely ready. There's always more money to be saved or more adventures to be had before having kids, but if you keep waiting, you'll never have them. Which is . . . also, a perfectly acceptable choice."

"I know. I do want them. This isn't me putting it off forever. It's just . . . it's a huge step and I'm terrified we'll screw the kid up, especially since it'll be an older kid."

"Older? You're not going to adopt a baby?" she asked as she took another small sip of her cabernet.

"No, no babies. I'd like them to be old enough to go to the bathroom on their own. Plus, older kids get overlooked a lot and I hate that. Although, if Ryan had his way, we'd get a teeny tiny baby, but he agreed to compromise with me on that decision. I'd say we're on the same page with age, just not timing."

"Well, whatever their age, it will be a major change in your household. Are you ready for that? For someone else to be there *all* the time? For them to rely on you for food, clothes, entertainment, money, and safety?"

"Well, when you put it like that . . ." he laughed and then suddenly got quiet. His pause spoke volumes. "Honestly, I don't know."

"Well, you need to know and you need to be 500% sure about your decision before you move forward. You might have to do the thing all married couples avoid . . . you're going to have to have an uncomfortable conversation with your husband."

JC rolled his eyes at her and moaned, before he dumped his head into his hands.

"Seriously though, you need to talk to Ryan. You need to be honest with him and explain what you're feeling. If I never give you advice again, just remember this, you have to communicate every . . . single . . . day. Even when you're mad, tired, sad, frustrated, happy, whatever. You just need to talk to each other and keep those lines of communication open at all costs. Try to keep your cool and don't get too emotional. And remember, you're talking to someone you love more than anything else in this world . . . so be respectful and understanding."

JC stared at Willa, giving her a look she couldn't decipher. He tapped his finger against the tile floor but gave her no indication that he heard her or planned to respond. She finally lifted her eyebrows in question and leaned sideways to put her face into his almost far-off vision. He finally snapped back to reality and spoke,

"Ugh, I hate that you're right."

"Seriously, what was that? You just sat there, staring and quiet and then that's what you responded with."

"I had to process what you said," he replied back, a confused look in his eyes.

She let out an exasperated laugh before she eyeballed her long-time friend and said, "Just don't do that to Ryan when you talk to him. Please. You'll fare much better if you don't."

JC stuck his tongue out at her and took another large sip of his wine.

"Whatever. I'll do my best. Anyways, what are all these papers? They came out of Steve's office?"

Willa released out a long sigh, "Yeah, plus these."

She handed him a stack of papers over an inch thick.

"These came out of a hidden drawer *under* Steve's desk. They look a lot like the other documents, but obviously they meant something special to him since they were kept in secret. I need to focus on all the other stuff though before I look into them. Maybe knowing what everything else is will help me understand what these say."

JC's head moved back and forth as he watched an almost-overwhelmed Willa, "I don't envy you for a second. I hate financial documents and this scenario reminds me a lot of the meeting I had with Trevor before he told me the bad news about my club. Speaking of, he set up an interview with a potential business partner tomorrow afternoon. I'm dreading that conversation, too. When did life get so damn hard?"

They shared a sad laugh, exchanged a knowing look, and then drained their wine glasses.

JC poured them each another glass and their laughter began to fill the room as they both drifted into a sillier and drunker state with each ruby red sip.

"Ugh," JC pulled his eyes open and groaned in pain. He lifted his face from the cold tile floor and rolled onto his back.

"I think I might . . . be dying," he said to no one in particular. He looked around, pulled off a piece of paper stuck to his cheek with a "rift" sound and rubbed away the dried drool on his lips. He blinked a few more times to get his contacts into focus and saw Willa leaning up against the smashed reception desk to his left.

"What are you doing?" he asked, his voice dry and husky.

She ignored him as her attention darted from a handful of papers in her left hand to a handful of papers in her right. JC's head throbbed and his mouth was as dry as the desert in the noontime sun. He cleared his froggy throat and tried again, louder this time, "Willa, what are you doing?"

She jumped at the sound of his voice and looked over at him, eyes wild and far away.

"I might have figured it out," she exclaimed, offering no other information.

JC shook his head and squeezed his eyes shut tight. It hurt his brain to think about, well anything, so he ignored her and focused on finding his phone and a mammoth-sized glass water.

He pulled himself to stand and fought off the urge to scream as his head pounded like an overworked jackhammer and threatened to actually crack open. Once he accepted the fact that his brains might drop out on the floor in front of him and how that might be a better feeling than the pressure-cooker sensation he had going on right now, he scanned the tile for his wayward phone.

He spotted it across the floor, plugged into an outlet, and lugged his cement-like feet towards the device. He experienced another possible brain explosion as he leaned down to pick up the stupid,

stupid phone. Once the pain subsided to a dull ache, he swiped up to unlock the screen and saw he had over 15 missed calls from Ryan and a slew of texts to go with his multiple voicemails. It dawned on him that he didn't go home last night and didn't let Ryan know his whereabouts. He sucked in a painful gasp and called out to Willa.

"I gotta go. I'm in such deep shit."

He started to run towards the front door but slowed when he realized his brain couldn't handle that kind of jostling in its current inflamed state.

"Uhh and I'm never drinking wine with you again!"

He didn't wait for her to reply, nor did he hear what she said when she yelled out after him. He got to his car and found a mostly full water bottle in his cup holder. Not worrying about how old the glorious liquid was, he downed it in a few huge gulps and slowly started to feel his body return to a state of not dead. He feared he might not feel normal again for a while after that wine-fueled rager of a night and began the uneasy ride home to face his husband.

"I'm so sorry," he called out as he barged through the front door. "I'm a terrible person and I owe you big time for staying out all night, but I think you should really blame Willa."

Maybe not a good time for jokes, he winced.

He poked his head into the empty kitchen and turned and bounded down the hall to the living room, even though his hangover still clung on for dear life. He saw Ryan working at his desk in the office off their living room and knocked on the French doors between them. This sent Sailor into a jumping fit.

Ryan swirled around in his computer chair and the look on his face made JC's stomach drop. He was in trouble and he knew it.

He pushed open the glass-framed door and practically crept into the room.

"Hi, babe. I'm really sorry." He didn't even try and sugarcoat his apology or make excuses. "I should have called or texted and I know you're mad and you have every right to be."

Ryan held up a hand and then said, "Willa texted me after you passed out. She said your phone was dead and that you were with her at the shelter and that she didn't want me to worry in case you had forgotten to message me. She even found a charger and plugged your phone in for you."

His face dropped its hard edge and he reached out for JC's hand. "She's a good friend. I'm glad you didn't drive, but I would have preferred to hear from you that you were staying out all night. Not her."

"I know and I'm sorry. I really am. I don't know what got into me. I don't usually guzzle wine like that. If it makes you feel any better, I do have a monstrous hangover. I feel like there's a giant hammer sticking out of my skull. There isn't, right?"

Ryan gave him a small smile, but it didn't reach his eyes.

"It does help a little," he said and then quieter, "But I have a feeling I know why you drank so much last night."

JC gave him a quizzical look, staying quiet so he could explain.

"You don't want to adopt. You aren't ready and I freaked you out with my declaration that I want to start the process next month."

JC watched his husband but didn't reply. His voice was frozen in his throat and his mind stalled, like an old, broken down 6-speed on the side of the road.

"But I don't care," Ryan continued, his voice growing stronger with every word and his body language morphing from meek mouse to confident king of the jungle lion. "I have put off starting my restaurant while you invested in your club for years and years. I've supported you with all your dreams and aspirations. You volunteer at the shelter, run events for them, and ask for my help to cater their functions. And I never complain. But you know what?"

His hand motions matched his words and he held up a finger for a second to emphasize his point and then dropped his hand to his sides as he said, "I'm done. I'm ready for it to be my turn. I want this and I need you to get on board, whether you're scared or not."

JC felt his surprise morph into anger as he listened to the sharp words that came out of his husband's normally calm mouth.

"But what if I can't? What if I'm not ready? What if I need more time? All I'm asking for is more time." JC questioned.

"I don't have any more time to give, JC. We agreed months . . . no, years ago, that this is where our lives were heading and that this was our timeframe."

"Our timeframe wasn't next month. You're pushing me on this and I'm not ready yet."

"If we take the classes next month, we won't be able to be matched with any kids until we're licensed and that won't be for another two or three months, at least. So, no, I'm not moving anything up. March is well-within our predetermined time frame." Ryan debated back.

"Well, what if I changed my mind? What if that timeframe doesn't work for me anymore?" JC questioned, feeling himself being backed into a corner.

"Have you? Is that what you're saying?" Ryan asked, his words almost aggressive.

"Yes. I've been saying that this entire discussion. I need more time. I'm not ready and I don't want to start the stupid classes next month." JC spit the words at Ryan, his emotions getting the better of him as his heart thumped hard inside his chest and pumped hot irate blood through his veins.

Ryan's eyes cut through JC's as his chest rose and fell in anger. He shook his head in disbelief before saying, "This is the one thing I've asked of you. The one thing . . ."

His voice was jarringly calm and JC was sure he could feel the disappointment radiating from his husband's skin. The disappointment in him and in their marriage . . . but he couldn't bring himself to speak.

He knew he agreed to the timeline and that he promised Ryan they'd grow their family together someday, but his mind was a mess right now and everything seemed so tangled up together.

His voice was frozen in his throat as he watched Ryan get up from his chair and grab his jacket before he blew past JC and walked out without saying anything more. The door slammed behind him and shook the walls of the house, along with the walls of their marriage.

JC spent the next few hours nursing his hangover and his pride. He cooked himself a carb-fueled breakfast in hopes that it'd help soak up the wine still fermenting in his stomach. He brewed an extra strong pot of coffee and sat down at the kitchen island to work on sorting out his current mess of a life. Sailor was his ever-constant shadow, who sat near him and followed him from room to room.

He wanted a family with Ryan, just not yet and he wanted to go through the foster-to-adopt classes with him too . . . just not yet. He didn't know what was holding him back though. What was the fear that was keeping him from moving forward with their adoption plans? Why couldn't he bring himself to say yes, when that's all his husband had ever asked of him?

Ryan was the best partner in the world. He and JC were a perfect match and they rarely fought, let alone storm out on each other. JC's actions lately had been out of character for him, like drinking and staying out all night, refusing to accept help at the club until the last minute, and pushing back against Ryan on the adoption plan. Why was he putting his marriage through the ringer like this? Why was he acting like someone he wasn't and why was he afraid of becoming a dad?

JC contemplated all these things and more while he sipped his coffee and got ready for his business meeting later that day. Fears, insecurities, and anxieties flew in and out of his brain all morning as he tried to make sense of his predicament. By the time he was at the club waiting for his meeting with his new potential business partner, he felt more paralyzed by fear than ever before.

A knock on the door brought JC out of his head and back to reality. He jumped off his chair and hurried over to welcome a pretty blonde-haired woman in her early-to-mid thirties into the club.

"Hi, I'm Ashley," she said in a southern drawl as she stretched out her hand to greet him.

Feeling immediately at ease with this woman, he reached out and returned her handshake.

"Hi, welcome to Spinners. I'm JC. Thanks for coming in today."

She released his hand and squatted to the floor to greet the ever-present Sailor, who danced in circles for her attention. The two exchanged kisses and pets and from their interaction, JC could tell she was a dog-lover, which made him like her even more.

JC ushered Ashley over to the bar before he gave her a tour of the club. He motioned to the large banquet room towards the back of the building, "So, this is where I think our events could be held, such as weddings or company parties. And off the back of this room is a large, outdoor patio that overlooks the bay. I have it decorated with lights and stuff, but I'm sure it could use a spruce from a new set of eyes."

Ashley smiled and looked around the room.

"It's a great space and there's a lot you could do with it. Even more than just weddings and company parties. I could see hosting custom bachelor and bachelorette parties, receptions and showers for weddings, babies, retirements . . . you name it, we could host it here. Plus, the outside space is great and we could charge more if they wanted to add that to their event—almost like concierge event planning. You start with the basic order of the room rental and add on from there. If they want food, drinks, nicer chairs, satin tablecloths, a private DJ, or the outdoor space, then the price goes up. If all that goes well, down the line, you could add marine options, such as trips out on a boat or floating tables for guests to cool off in the water on hot summer days."

JC caught himself staring at Ashley as she spouted off these ideas like they just came to her. These were things he'd never think about in a million years and he had no idea how to incorporate them into his business. Even more, he had no desire to plan or execute them. If she had the experience and chops to pull that off, she might have just earned herself part ownership in his club.

Their meeting went on for another two hours, but JC missed most of it as he found himself lost in his thoughts about Ryan and their fight. He pulled himself back into the meeting with Ashley on numerous occasions without knowing much of what was said before, but he hoped it was just fluff and typical interview crap.

"So, do you have any other questions for me?" Ashley asked, a smile on her face but a questioning look in her eye.

"Sorry, if I've been a little unfocused. I just have a lot on my mind."

She nodded and gave him an understanding look as he continued, "Trevor told me that he explained the business's financial woes to you and I just wanted to ask, why doesn't it bother you or scare you off?"

"Because I know all businesses go through ups and downs when they're trying to find their way. Plus, I've done my homework, so I know that Ocean Park and the surrounding area doesn't have a club like the one we'd create if we partnered together. With your experience as a bar and dance club manager, you could easily add some different bands to the schedule and turn this place into the next hot spot for touring acts when they come through Eastern Maryland. They could go north from here to Dover, Delaware or west to the suburbs of DC or Baltimore. Plus, add in my part of the business and we could become the events mecca for the eastern seaboard." She laughed and then added, "Or at least for our little area of the beachside towns."

JC smiled as the wheels finally started turning in his head, "No, no, I like it! Dream big!"

All of a sudden, all his problems seemed more manageable as he and Ashley discussed their possible plans for the club. She showed him financial charts and projections and excitement oozed from her as she explained why she wanted to join his business.

After the formalities were out of the way, the two ended up talking for another half hour about their interests outside of work. Ashley explained that she moved to the area from Wilmington after meeting her boyfriend down here on vacation. They had just moved in together and she met Trevor, JC's accountant, through a business-networking group. She had a golden retriever mix, named Sebastian, who loved to swim in the ocean and hoped her business-owning boyfriend would propose soon since they had been together for almost a year, although it was mostly long distance. She talked about her past jobs and how she got into event planning and asked JC some similar questions, which he answered honestly since they might be in bed together soon—business wise.

JC talked about his baseball background, his love for the shelter animals, and his wonderful husband, Ryan. He heard himself go into detail about how he felt so lucky to have met Ryan and how he was so proud of him for working his ass off to create and grow his food truck and catering business. He felt himself smile as he explained to her the details of their wedding and how they worked together to help Ocean Pals during the difficult time after the break-in.

Ashley asked if they had any kids and JC's heart pounded hard in his chest. A voice inside his head screamed and he shook it side to side to silence it. So, he just smiled and said, "no", but the voice yelled again, louder this time. He struggled to give her a small smile as she explained that she loved kids and hoped to have three of her own someday. The voice in JC's head bellowed, almost screeching at him, causing his ears to ring and his brain to falter.

The words tumbled out of his mouth, like he couldn't control them—like they had a mind of their own. He completely interrupted Ashley, but she didn't seem to mind. An excited smile crossed over her face and she eagerly nodded at him.

"I'd like to move forward with this business partnership, if you're still on board."

And with those words, JC knew he had just created a new path for himself. And there was only one person he wanted to tell.

Chapter 15
MONROE and Emily

Steve groaned as he opened his eyes and joined the conscious world again. His whole body hurt and every nerve ending screamed in pain. Footsteps from his left caught his attention and he looked towards the noise. Marco, Chris's right hand man, came at him full steam and landed another swift kick across his lower back. Steve pulled his large body into a ball and tried hard not to scream out in pain as shockwaves of agony tore through his bones.

"And that's one for the road, you son of a bitch," Marco spat. "Chris expects his money within 48 hours or else you, and all these worthless animals, will go up in smoke."

The words ripped through Steve's ears and it was a threat he knew Chris and Marco would keep if he didn't comply with their demands. He kept his mouth shut and hoped they'd leave as fast as they came.

"There's a reminder on the wall if you fucking forget," Marco said with a laugh before he whistled to the rest of his men. "Let's get outta here, boys!"

Steve listened as the men clamored out of the building, breaking more windows, and shaking their cans of spray paint as they went. The clanging and banging became quiet and Steve was left alone with all his animals, bloody and beaten.

He hauled himself up to sit and looked around the lobby through his already-swollen eyes. The place was a disaster. He strained to listen harder and could hear whimpering through the barrage of dog barking. He moved to stand and let out a wrenching cry, as the pain in his left knee was almost unbearable. He pushed through and hobbled to the dog kennels, where he saw all the dogs inside their cages except for Hollywood and Caleb. They were both in the open hallway between the two rows of kennels, somehow out of their cages. Caleb looked unconscious or dead, while Hollywood stared at him with terrified eyes, crying in pain.

Overwhelmed at the sight, he pushed into the room and checked on Caleb first, to see if he was even alive. He was and Steve lifted his body back into his cage but left his kennel door open. He did the same with Hollywood and then staggered out of the shelter to his car. He had to get the money and he had to get it now.

Emily couldn't believe she was at a casino in the middle of the night while her dogs and cats at the shelter were suffering. She looked over at the man responsible for bringing her into this mess and fought the urge to wring his neck.

Steve came to her one night a few years ago distraught and almost hysterical. He had lost a bunch of money gambling and needed a loan before he got in too deep with his bookie. Emily offered him a one-time loan. As a former addict herself, she knew how addiction could creep into every aspect of your life and begin to unravel even your best laid plans.

That one-time loan came and went and the next thing she knew, Steve was borrowing money from the shelter to pay back his debts.

"Why didn't I turn him in then?" She questioned herself as she watched him lose another hand of poker and slam his hand down against the table in defeat.

She rolled her eyes and remembered why.

Steve had promised her a spot on the shelter's board of directors, explaining that she could do even more good for the animals as a member of the board. He also guaranteed that if he ever stepped down as shelter director, that she would be the next one in line to take over the job.

Emily would do anything for the animals at the shelter. They had helped her recover from the deepest hole she ever dug for herself. After falling off the wagon at AA for the third time, she started volunteering at Ocean Pals and found her purpose in helping animals. She dragged herself back to AA and stayed sober for the last 20 years with the help of the program and the help of the animals. They needed her as much as she needed them. So, the promise of being an even bigger help to them was incredibly tempting to her.

Steve validated his actions by making large donations to the shelter under a pseudonym the few times he had hit it big at the casino. We're not just talking $500 or $1,000 donations, either. He would hit the jackpot and then donate $25,000, which was a lot to a shelter that didn't get any government funding.

This time, he took it too far though and if he couldn't get the money back, she was going to go to the police. She knew she'd get in trouble too, for helping him falsify the finances to the other members of the board of directors, but she didn't care. It was her cross to bear and all she cared about now was getting the money and getting back to the shelter to help with clean up.

They'd been at the casino for the past 36 hours and Steve only had 12 hours left to get the money to pay back Chris. They'd spent $10,000, but had made back $25,000, so they had another $25,000 to go. Loud cheering at the next table caught her attention and she looked over to see Steve jumping up and down in celebration.

He looked over to her and gave her a thumbs up before holding up his 10 thick fingers, signaling he'd just won another $10,000.

Make that $15,000 more to go.

After another 4 long hours at the casino, Steve had lost another $10,000 and was back to needing to make up another $25k. Emily had made $5,000 but was keeping it to herself so he didn't go and lose that money too.

"We only have 8 hours left," Emily squirmed, as she bit at her nails.

"If I can't get the money, what do you have in the bank that you can get a hold of fast?" Steve asked as sweat ran down his round face.

Emily shook her head firmly, "Nothing. I'm not bailing you out of this one, Steve. Not again."

He turned to her with shock written all over his face, "How can you say that? The animals need this money. They'll hurt them again if you don't help me."

"Stop using the animals against me when you're the one whose losing all their money. You know what? You're on your own now. I'm out."

While Steve yelled after her, she turned and walked out of the casino and headed straight for the shelter.

"Where have you been? Are you okay? Do you know where Steve is?"

Emily was berated with questions as she entered the shelter.

"Willa, calm down. I was out of town and my phone died," she lied. "I came back as soon as I got it charged and heard what happened. How are the dogs who were hurt?"

"Hollywood is recovering well. He needed lots of stitches, but had no internal bleeding, broken bones, or brain bleeds. Caleb is in rough shape. He has a fractured front paw, a small bleed in his brain from a significant concussion, and a missing tooth. The brain bleed is under control for now, but he needs to be under close medical care for a few more weeks. Hollywood is expected to go to his temporary foster home next week."

Emily breathed a slight sigh of relief for Hollywood, but her heart broke for Caleb.

"Do they think Caleb will ever be okay?"

"They're hopeful he'll make a full recovery but are erring on the side of caution since he had such a major blow to the head. We're staying positive."

Rage flowed through Emily's body as she thought about Caleb's injuries and the man who brought them upon him. She blamed Steve for all of this, regardless if he was the one who attacked Caleb or not. Trying to keep her cool, she focused on what was in front of her now.

"What's all of this?"

She watched as Willa fumbled around with different documents that surrounded her on the floor.

"These are the financials for the shelter. The board asked me to go over them when they couldn't get a hold of you or Steve. I can't make sense of them yet, but what I can make sense of is something shady is going on."

"What do you mean?" Emily asked, faking surprise.

"Money is being moved around left and right and most of it is duplicated every month. Food costs will be noted in the expenses ledger and then there will be another note for it in the miscellaneous section. Why the two entries?"

"Maybe they didn't have enough that month?" Emily tried. "Sometimes we run out and need to make extra orders."

"But every single month?" Willa asked. "It doesn't make sense. And that's not the only thing."

She pulled a bunch of papers from a red folder and handed them to Emily.

"Have you ever seen these?"

Emily opened the folder and scanned the pages. Names of dogs that they had adopted out showed up on the page, but in a column to the right was a DOB and a DOD . . . date of birth and date of death.

"What is this? We adopted these dogs out. They *all* died already?" Emily's voice shook with concern.

"No," Willa said.

Her normal stoic face was worn and tired and with sad eyes, she looked up at Emily.

"Look, I've been here all night going over these documents. They all came out of Steve's office. They were in a locked cabinet hidden under his desk and I guess when the break-in happened the other night, they got jostled loose."

The look on Emily's face showed that she never knew about the secret cabinet and she pressed Willa to continue.

"You know how we never saw the adoption photos of some of the dogs who were "adopted" and we just sort of thought it was because someone forgot to get one or the family didn't want it online or whatever?"

Emily nodded.

When a dog or cat was adopted, they always asked if they could get a photo of the pet with their new family before they pranced off to their forever home. They'd post the pictures on Ocean Pals' Facebook and Instagram pages with a happy caption celebrating the pet's official "gotcha" day.

"Well, all those dogs are on this list." Willa looked pained as she explained the next part. "And from what I'm seeing here, it looks like Steve ... put them all down instead and just told everyone he adopted them out."

Emily felt her legs give out and she slumped to the floor. She pulled the folder back up to where she could read the names and tried to wrap her head around Willa's explanation.

"No, that can't be. He'd never do that."

She stuttered as tears welled up and fell from her tired eyes.

"Oh no," she clapped her hand over her mouth. "Indiana. My boy, Hunk, and Karla . . . oh my god."

She read the names of the dogs she thought were in their forever homes, living long, happy lives. As she sobbed, she read the last name on the list and brought her eyes to Willa.

"Monroe?" she cried. "Monroe's gone? He was so sweet. Oh no, no. All these dogs were so sweet. So nice and so perfect. They didn't deserve to die. Why would he do this?"

Willa didn't answer right away and let Emily cry for a minute before she answered.

"There was another document in that folder with reasons for his decision. For Karla, it was that she had a failed adoption and had been here too long."

Emily interjected, "But, we don't care how long they've been here? We don't put anyone down for that!" Her voice was loud and emotional.

Willa nodded with a sad frown spread across her face, "I know. We don't, but I guess Steve does. Indiana was because of her ongoing skin condition and he didn't want to invest in her medication any longer."

Emily shook her head but couldn't bring herself to speak. Her heart was broken and she didn't believe this catastrophe could get any worse.

But it had.

"Monroe was put down because he barked too much. On the paper it just said, in capital letters, TOO LOUD."

Emily squeezed her eyes shut and willed her body to wake up from this horrible dream. Monroe was the sweetest hound dog she'd ever met. Yeah, of course he barked in his kennel, but when he was out in the yard or on a walk, he was perfect, quiet, and sweet. He loved to swim, chase the ball, and stayed perfectly beside you on his walks. He just needed time to find the right family who loved and understood hound dogs and their vocal nature.

Her body quaked with sobs as she mourned for her babies—ones she loved and thought were off living the good life. Only to find out they were dragged to the back room, terrified and alone, where Steve, her former best friend, would stick a needle in their trembling, healthy bodies and end their lives.

Right then and there she vowed to take him down. To make him pay for everything he had done.

"Willa," her voice creaked but her eyes stayed firm, "All of this is Steve's fault."

She gestured with her hands to the destruction of the shelter, "He's the reason someone broke in and hurt the dogs. This is all his fault and I can prove it."

Willa shook her head and looked at Emily with confused eyes, "What do you mean? What do you know?"

Emily wiped away her hot tears and lifted her head high, "Everything. You might want to call the detectives. They'll want to hear this too."

Chapter 16
MILEY and Sammi

Sammi's stomach was in knots and those knots were doing round off back handsprings over and over again. She had just finished her makeup for her coffee date with Trevor and was giving herself one last once over before she headed downstairs to grab her purse and leave. They were meeting at the coffee shop in downtown Ocean Park. Trevor had offered to pick her up, but since she hadn't explained that she still lived at home with her mother at 35, she insisted they drive separately.

As her feet hit the last step, her mom called out from her spot next to the wood-burning fireplace. She always sat in a baby blue, high-backed chair when she read her romance novels. She was halfway through her newest one but put it down and catcalled to her daughter.

"Woohoo, girl, you look great!" Ruth encouraged as Sammi did a little spin.

"I love the purple sweater on you."

Her smile brightened Sammi's nervous mood and released the tension in her shoulders enough to allow her to take a long, deep breath. A much-needed breath.

Sammi's outfit of tight, dark jeans, her already mentioned purple sweater, and black boots with a small heel felt good on her body. She knew the sweater was dark enough to hide any nervous sweat stains she might get under her arms and her jeans were comfortable but stretchy, so they had that skintight, sexy look that she wanted, but she could still actually sit down in them without muffin-topping over the sides.

She grabbed her purse from the end table next to the couch and checked her phone for the time. She still had 15-minutes to wait before she could leave and not be obnoxiously early. That was another reason she hated first dates—you had to get all ready and then wait, all nervous and twitchy, for the damn thing to start. Waiting was the worst and the anticipation always felt like it was going to kill her.

Sammi and Ruth chitchatted for another 10 excruciating minutes before Sammi couldn't bear it anymore and stood to leave . . . five minutes before her already generous allotted leave time.

"Aren't you going to be early?" Ruth chuckled as she watched Sammi struggle to pack her phone into her tiny purse.

"Yeah, but you know how I hate being late."

"I don't think there's a chance in hell that you could be late if you leave now. You'd have to stop and have a full meal, maybe even see a few movies, for you to be late," her mom joked.

"Ha ha. I know I'll be early, but this way I'll be able to find a parking spot, check my makeup once last time, and give myself a pep talk before I go in. Plus, I'll be able to find a good spot inside if he's not there yet. It's my nervous routine, Mom, you know I'm weird about these things."

Ruth just smiled and nodded at her daughter. She was used to her nervous-nelly behaviors and her dependence on her "routines."

Maybe a boyfriend and a little hot sex will help her relax a bit, she thought to herself as Sammi walked to the door.

Sammi turned to look at her mom one more time with her hand on the doorknob, "Why are you smiling?"

Ruth shook her head, "No reason, honey. Have a good time and give the guy a chance."

Sammi groaned and pulled the heavy door open, "I will, I promise."

And with that, she was off for her date with the sexpot accountant, Trevor.

At the coffee shop, Sammi tapped her foot and felt her eyes shoot to the door every five seconds or so. To terrorize her more, the knots in her stomach had released a whole swarm of butterflies and she was pretty sure she could feel every single drop of sweat as it poured out of her armpits.

When a figure walking to the door caught her eye, she focused in on it and saw that it was Trevor. He looked handsome in his jeans and buttoned up shirt. Very stylish but casual. The butterflies noticed too and swarmed a little harder.

Her heart caught in her chest and she felt a smile pull at her lips. He came through the door of the shop smiling and his eyes were fixated on her. She stood up to meet him and as they walked towards each other, her purse strap wrangled itself around the back of a chair and like a scene in a movie, it toppled over in a loud crash that brought everyone's eyes to them.

Sammi felt her face get hot and could only imagine that the deep shade of crimson spreading across her skin was probably clashing with her dark purple sweater. She scrambled to pick up the chair and untangled herself from its grasp, just as Trevor did the same. He moved to her in his long, graceful stride and bent down to help her stand up, concern spread across his handsome face.

"Are you alright?" he asked as his hand grabbed hers. His dark chocolate skin contrasted against her light freckled tone and all she could think about were the lightning bolts shooting between their skin as he touched her.

"Yeah, I'm fine. Sorry, I'm such a klutz. You'll learn that about me."

He gave her a funny look, "But weren't you a gymnast?"

"Yeah, that doesn't stop me from being a complete moron with two left feet in real life though. Put me on a four-foot high, four-inch wide balance beam and I'm golden, but down here, in the real world, I'm nothing sort of a disaster."

He laughed and smiled at her words before it dawned on her that she never told him about her gymnastics past.

"Wait, how did you know that about me?" She asked, trying not to sound accusatory, just curious.

Now it was his turn to feel the wrath of embarrassment and he rubbed the back of his head with his hand, "Um, busted. I talked to JC about you."

He gave her an apologetic look, "But he didn't tell me too much. Just a few basic things. It was his idea. When he heard about our date, he started texting me little facts about you. I think he's super excited we're out together."

Sammi laughed and shook her head, "That sounds like something JC would do. What did he tell you?"

"Just that you were a gymnast and that you're a coach now. That your favorite color is purple, which by the way," he looked her up and down, "You look wonderful. He also said that you were in a long-term relationship a while ago. Oh, and that you don't eat meat."

Sammi bit her lip in hopes to hide her silly grin, "Thank you. You look great too. Very dashing. And that's basically all there is to know about me. The major chunks at least."

"I'm sure there's more than that," He said with a wink.

They moved away from the area of the fallen chair fiasco and took a few steps over to the counter. Sammi watched as he ordered his coffee and she felt a flash of exhilaration swim through her body. She knew in the first few minutes of her last first dates that it was never going to work out with those guys, but this time, she felt hope, excitement, and desire towards the hunk of a man standing next to her.

Is this what it feels like to be on a good first date? She thought to herself.

Trevor's hand on her shoulder brought her out of her thoughts.

"What would you like to drink?" he asked as her eyes moved from his touch to his caramel eyes.

Oh yeah, this is a good first date for sure. I could get used to this, she said to herself before offering her coffee order to the waiting barista.

Two hours and two empty coffee mugs later, Trevor and Sammi decided to take their date from the coffee shop to the beach for a walk. Trevor grabbed her hand as they left the building and smiled at her as they walked towards the sand that was a few blocks away.

"So, I have something to tell you," she said, as she fell in line with his long stride.

"Uh oh, what's up?" he asked, his voice kind and curious.

"This is super embarrassing, but I think you should know before we get any more involved."

His expression turned to one of concern and he waited for her to continue.

"After my ex and I broke up, I didn't have anywhere to go. So, I moved in with my mom ... and I still live there."

The words came out choppy and doused in remorse. She watched his face as he digested the words and was surprised when his reaction wasn't what she expected.

He gave her a nonchalant shrug and little smile, "Okay. That's cool."

"Wait, you don't think it's weird that I'm 35 years old and still live at home with my mom?"

"Well, I wouldn't say that it's ideal, but it's not like you never left. You're just there while you get back on your feet. There's no harm in that. We all go through struggles."

Sammi's heart swelled for the man who walked next to her. His honest and accepting reaction to her odd living situation fueled her desire for him even more. *Talk about a catch.*

"If we're talking about possible hang ups to this relationship moving forward, then I have something to tell you too."

Dammit, spoke too soon, Sammi thought as she waited for his announcement.

"Even though I'm a business-owner and accountant, I'm in debt up to my eyeballs. I took out a lot of loans for school and then while I was paying those down, my ex-wife ran up our credit cards. She took out any card she could get her hands on and I didn't know about most of them. Once I realized what she was doing, that was the straw that broke the proverbial camel's back and I asked for a divorce. We had other issues prior to that."

He paused but didn't elaborate on the "other issues." Best to stick to one major revelation per date.

"But when I did that, she started taking loans out in our names without my permission and now I'm left with half of those debts too. So, that's my Achilles' heel. I'm 39 and in a massive amount of debt."

Sammi's eyebrows wanted to react and her face wanted to contort and ask a bunch of questions like, "How didn't you know?" and "Why do you have to pay them back if she did it without your knowledge?" and "Exactly, how much debt are we talking about?" but she knew the right thing to do was nod, keep her mouth shut, and wait to find out those extra details later.

Except she was terrible at hiding her emotions and Trevor noticed a shift in her attitude almost immediately.

"Look, I know it's a lot to take in. I understand if you don't want to see me anymore because it is a major hurdle I have to manage, but I'm working on pulling myself out of the foxhole."

"No, no, I want to keep seeing you. I just need a moment to digest it, I guess," she lied.

Her desire and optimism about the future with Trevor dribbled away as she thought more about his situation. She just started putting money in her savings account again now that she was out from under the thumb of her ex's extravagant lifestyle. How would they make it work if she was a deadbeat living at home and he was a deadbeat living in debt? What would they be, two deadbeats living in her mom's house forever? She was hoping for a different relationship, not one that started off with them both struggling from the get-go.

Fortunately for him, something else caught her attention and she pointed down the unoccupied beach at one of the few lifeguard chairs still out on the sand. A small, dark figure was huddled up next to the chair, but Sammi couldn't make out what it was at that distance.

"What is that?" She asked as she squinted at the far-off image.

They walked a little faster and Trevor stared for a few seconds before he said, "I think it might be a dog."

They looked at each other and then took off running. They reached the huge wooden stand at the same time and saw that someone tied their old, German shepherd to one of the posts. The dog looked deflated, tired, cold, and dejected. She let out a long cry as they stood there looking at her, with open mouths and breaking hearts.

The dog's cry tore through Sammi's gut. You could hear the desperation and longing for her former family in her howls. Her emotion was evident in her stance, as her head hung low and her tail stuck tightly under her belly. She looked older, maybe 11, and for a larger dog like a German shepherd, that's getting up there.

Sammi crouched down and talked quietly to the dog. She reached her hand out to let her sniff her scent, but the dog ignored her. She released another blood curdling cry and then threw her head back and howled to the sky before her eyes came back to the same spot they were on before. She looked in the direction that her old owner would have left the beach. Footsteps could be seen in the sand and the old dog watched, hopeful that they'd return for her.

Sammi moved closer to the dog and gently stroked her head. Her fur was wiry and wet. She didn't acknowledge Sammi and stood stoic in her position. Sammi was able to turn her collar so her tags were behind her head instead of in front of her, where, if she wanted to, she could easily grab

Sammi's hand with her teeth. Sammi read her name from her lone tag. Miley.

"Hi, Miley," she said, and the dog's ears turned towards her. Miley didn't dare look at her but Sammi could tell that she got her attention.

Trevor walked around them and untied the leash knotted to the lifeguard stand. Once she was free, Sammi tried again.

"Miley. Hey, girl. Do you want to come with us? It's cold out here and we can take you somewhere safe and warm."

The dog lifted her head and turned it to Sammi. She threw her head back again and wailed into the salty air.

"I know, baby. I know you're sad and scared. But, we're here to help." She said through the lump in her throat. She was fighting back tears—Tears that threatened to fall from the sadness that radiated from Miley and from anger at her owner for dumping her there. They obviously had a connection for her to be this depressed.

Trevor cleared his throat and Sammi looked back at him as he wiped his hand over his face. This was getting to him too.

"Miley," he tried, his voice quiet over the loud waves that crashed behind them. "Come on, sweet girl. Come with us. We'll take care of you."

His voice seemed to activate her and she turned to look at him. She took her first steps and moved towards him. He had her leash, so he waited for her to sniff him before he reached down and scratched her head. She let out another round of heartbreaking cries and then began to follow Trevor to the road.

The three of them walked together, back towards the coffee shop as Miley barked, howled, and cried the whole way. Her heartbreak at being abandoned was clear to everyone they passed and some people stared, some held their hands up to their mouths in empathy, and others simply looked the other way, just like her owner did when they left her alone on the beach, crying and wailing in pain.

Trevor loaded Miley into his truck and he and Sammi agreed to meet at the shelter. They hoped someone there would know what to do with her, even though they were still working on repairs after the break-in.

"How was the ride over?" Sammi asked Trevor as they walked to the blue Ocean Pals building.

"She curled into the tightest, smallest ball and didn't move a muscle until we got here. As soon as

I put the truck into park, she popped up so fast that she startled me. She was so intense and looked out the window scanning the nearby buildings like she was looking for her home. I guess, when she didn't see it, she just slumped her head and it stayed hanging low. She lets out little whimpers and cries every so often. I can't believe some asshole would just leave her. How could you walk away while your dog was crying and barking for you like that? I just don't get it."

He was visibly shaken by the emotional trauma Miley felt and Sammi was grateful she rode to the shelter in her own car. She was sure she couldn't have handled that and knew she would have been moved to blubbery tears if she had to watch Miley get excited and then fall apart, all over again, when she realized she wasn't at home.

They entered the building and found the detectives investigating the break-in leaving as they walked up to the freshly installed reception desk. Willa came over to them after she walked the detectives out.

"What's up, guys? Who is this?" she asked and bent down to meet Miley, who ignored her.

"This is Miley. We found her tied up on the beach to one of those big lifeguard stands," Trevor said as Miley let out another emotional howl.

"Oh Miley, what's wrong?" Willa asked, her voice raising an octave or two as she sensed the old girl's sadness. She petted her for a few moments and tried to engage with her, but stood up when Miley continued to ignore her to cry. "Let's scan her for a microchip."

Willa pulled out a device that looked similar to an old Playboy game console. She held it over Miley's neck and then moved it around her upper body and front legs, waiting for it to activate.

"Over time their microchips can move. They put them in the back of their neck, sort of near their shoulder blades but we've had a few dogs and cats come in that had them in different places, like down their front legs or along their sides. So, we always check the whole body. It'll beep when it scans the chip."

Almost as if on cue, the detector beeped and Willa read the screen.

"It says her name is Miley, which we already know and it's giving me a number to enter into the company's website."

Willa walked around the reception desk and pulled up the site. She typed in the number and Miley's history popped up on the screen, including her picture and owner's information. Without hesitating for a second, Willa picked up the phone and dialed the owner's number.

Sammi watched her in awe as Willa moved through life with such confidence and drive. She didn't overthink everything and just went with her gut.

I wish I could be more like her, Sammi thought to herself. *I'd be terrified to call that owner and confront them.*

Willa left a voicemail and asked them to call her back at the shelter. She also gave them her cell number.

"If you ever have to do this when you volunteer here, give people multiple ways to contact you. Not a lot of people will call you back, but they might email or text you if you give them that option."

Trevor and Sammi nodded in understanding as Miley moaned out another howl.

Willa scratched her head and closed her eyes like she was deep in thought before she spoke, "I'm trying to think of who could take her in for a few days until we're able to open up the kennels again."

Her phone buzzed and she grabbed it, leaving her worries about who could foster Miley for the time being. She dropped her hand to her side and it slapped against her leg as she let out a long, irritated sigh.

"It looks like you're going to be with us for a while, sweetie," she said to Miley before she turned her attention to Trevor and Sammi. "That was her owner. They said they don't want her back."

"Did they say why?" Sammi asked, her voice harsh and emotional.

Willa shook her head, "Nope."

They all looked at each other with different emotions. Trevor looked pissed and crushed at the same time. It was obvious he felt bad for Miley. Sammi looked astonished and like she was on the verge of bawling. Willa looked forlorn but not surprised.

"This is a part of shelter life. We feel these raw emotions and we're heartbroken for the dogs, but you have to push through it, so it doesn't take over your life. Remember the good we do and think of how happy Miley will be when we find her a forever home. Try to stay positive."

Sammi fought back her tears and tried to take Willa's advice to heart. If she wanted to be more like her, then she needed to listen to her. Trevor grabbed her hand and gave it a tight squeeze as he looked down at her with pained eyes. She forced a smile at him and saw it eased his tension a little in the process. He smiled back at her and she felt the same tiny, sense of relief.

Sammi's heart broke for Miley, but in that moment, clarity washed over her when it came to Trevor. She was thinking of walking away before they found Miley. She had doubts she could handle his financial hurdles and wanted someone who wasn't as worse off as her. But seeing Miley wail for her owners and listening to Willa explain that she will be happy again once she learned to trust, turned Sammi's heart around.

I have to give Trevor a chance. I have to learn to trust again. So what if we're both trying to rebuild our lives. Maybe we can build them back up together.

Her thoughts were interrupted when Willa came over to them and bent down to talk to Miley.

"You're coming home with me. I hope you like other dogs. Us old gals gotta stick together."

And with that, Miley found herself a foster home and the words seemed to make sense to her. She took a few steps forward toward Willa, lifted her head, and gave her a small kiss on the nose.

"Baby steps, sweetie. Baby steps," Willa said through her smile.

She grabbed Miley's leash and thanked Sammi and Trevor for finding her and demanded they get back to their date.

"Get out of here, you two, before I put you to work. Have fun and come back tomorrow if you want to help us paint!"

She waved them off but they both looked back to Miley, who watched them go, her sad eyes following them out the door.

Chapter 17
VITO and Willa

Willa watched Trevor and Sammi walk out the front door of the shelter, hand in hand, before she warned Miley that they couldn't go home until after her meeting with the Ocean Pal's Board of Directors.

They called this meeting after the cops arrested Emily. She gave them all the information they needed to arrest Steve for his embezzlement scheme from the shelter, but they hadn't been able to find him yet. The board of directors was frantically trying to understand how the situation had gotten so bad and how they were all misled for so long. They hoped to make some changes in the next meeting, or so that's what they told Willa when they asked her to meet.

The eight board members began arriving and all stopped to meet Miley before they went to check on the status of the shelter. The volunteers and employees had been working hard the last few days to get the shelter back into decent shape. They had a few more coats of paint to put on the walls and a construction crew was coming on Monday to finish fixing the condo area and some ornery fencing panels Trevor and Willa couldn't get to stay up.

When everyone was there, Jocelyn, the board president, called the meeting to order and asked Willa to explain the situation again—from the beginning, including how she figured it all out.

"Well, I found some hidden financial documents and details about some faked adoptions. They were very confusing and I spent most of that evening going over all the data to get a better grasp of what they were all about. Once I figured out that there was some double dipping going on with certain accounts, I followed the money to a miscellaneous account that was only sending money out to an unknown payee. It never showed any money coming in, so I figured it was a vendor account. I looked it up and couldn't find it in our register, so after some more digging and calls to our bank, I uncovered the name of the account holder. William Thompson. We don't have a contract with any vendor or person under that name, but I couldn't get anywhere else with it, so I moved on to some other documents."

She looked around at the faces listening intently to her and felt terrible about the news she had to deliver to them next.

"From those documents, I found that Steve was faking adoptions and euthanizing healthy, adoptable pets instead. He would tell you, me, and the other employees that a dog or cat was adopted, but that they forgot to get a picture or that he misplaced the paperwork when, in reality, he used his background as a vet tech to administer pentobarbital to the animals and put them to sleep. He always documented why and all of the reasons are not acceptable ones according to the bylaws here at Ocean Pals.

After discovering this, I was sort of at a dead end since the financials weren't leading me anywhere else, but I hit a break when Emily finally showed up to the shelter and I filled her in on what I knew so far. She asked me to call the detectives and laid out Steve's whole plan for us, without leaving anything out. Not even the information that ultimately led to her arrest. She was an accomplice in covering up his embezzlement and gambling problems, but she had no idea he was killing innocent animals. Learning about that is, in my opinion, what made her open up about his financial crimes."

"She used her power on the board to help lead you all astray and keep you from finding out about his stealing. She thought she was doing the right thing for the animals, but I believe she knows better now."

"As far as Steve, the cops are still looking for him. His wife has no idea where he is and they haven't been able to track his phone. His last location shows him pinging at an area off of Racetrack Road in Berlin, but all they found was his smashed cell phone."

"What they know from Emily is that he stole another $25,000 from the shelter before he went to the casino to try and double or triple it. Emily said he owed his bookie money and that they were the ones who broke into the shelter because he had missed a few months of payments. It was a warning. The last communication from his phone was a text to Emily saying, "I got it! I won all his money back and more! We're safe and in the clear.""

"Emily was in police custody at the time and never replied to the message and she never received another text from him before his phone went dark. The cop's theory is that when he didn't hear back from Emily, he ran off with the money and is laying low somewhere. They've put out a regional wide alert with all the authorities and are waiting to get a hit on his whereabouts. They're hopeful, but basically out of leads."

"How did this happen?" Justin, a senior board member asked, while the others nodded in agreement and turned their attention to Willa.

"Because we never ran out of money and because Steve would drop large donations back into our accounts from time to time. No one had any idea to look for something like this. Plus, with Emily helping him and his fine-tuned accounting skills and not a lot of oversight, it's not surprising it went on for so long unnoticed. He could have continued this scheme indefinitely if not for the break-in, which unearthed the euthanasia documents."

"How can we make sure it doesn't happen again?" Carlos, a newer board member asked.

Willa went into her spiel about how they could improve their financial management and should include more safeguards to deter things like this from happening in the future. The board hounded her with a few more questions and then asked her to step out while they deliberated amongst themselves.

She did as they asked and took Miley outside to stretch her legs and relieve her aging bladder. The two sat out together in the sun for 20 minutes, neither noticing the cold, before the board welcomed Willa back into their meeting.

"We've discussed it and all feel that the shelter needs a strong, trustworthy leader in the director position," Jocelyn said to Willa when she returned. She had an odd look on her face, almost mischievous, and Willa was focusing on that when Jocelyn finally said, "And we think that person should be you."

Willa felt her eyes shoot up in surprise at their suggestion. Not in a million years did she expect them to say her name. This was not a position she wanted, or ever thought about having, and her face must've been registering that look because the board members were all watching her with hesitant eyes.

"Wow, I didn't expect . . ." she stumbled. "Just wow. This, uh . . . are you sure?"

A few members chuckled at her shocked yet honest reaction before Carlos said, "Yes, we're sure. You've demonstrated that you're the hardest working, most reliable, and trustworthy volunteer here. With your financial background and understanding, plus your love for the animals, it's really a no brainer for us."

Willa smiled at the words but felt something pulling at her gut.

"Look, I really appreciate the confidence you have in me, but I have a lot going on in my home life right now and I'm not sure I can take on such a time-consuming role. I'm not saying no, but I have a counteroffer."

The board listened as she laid out her terms and conditions for accepting the position. It took all of five minutes for them to decide and vote on it, to which they unanimously agreed. Willa clapped her hands together and looked to Miley, who was resting by her side.

"We have a lot of work ahead of us, girl. Time to get started."

Willa was about to leave for the night when she realized that she needed to go to Emily's house and pick up Vito, her foster dog. Emily had asked her to take care of him since he was home alone and she was going right into police custody after her confession to the cops. Willa agreed since Emily was a huge help in uncovering Steve's crimes and she didn't want Vito to suffer any longer. He'd already been home alone for almost two days.

"Who could we get to foster him?" she asked Miley, who looked at her quizzically. The German shepherd just tilted her head to the side, while Willa tapped her finger to her lips in thought.

"Oh, I know. Maybe Thomas would take him," she exclaimed after a few minutes of brainstorming. "Oh, but that means I have to go there and talk to him about it."

She moaned and brought her head into her hands in an un-like-her dramatic fashion before she pulled herself back together.

"You're right. I gotta do what I gotta do. It's for the good of the shelter. And now that I'm a director, I need to do all I can . . . even if that means interacting with my ex-husband."

Miley barked in response and Willa winked at the older dog and started to gather her things.

"Let's go, girl. I'll drop you off at home and then I'll get Vito and take him to Waves. Thomas won't be able to say no once he sees him."

She and Miley made the short drive to her house and when they walked up the deck to go through the front door, they saw Baylor and Dalton sitting at the outdoor table on the wrap around porch.

"Hey, what are you guys doing out here? You won't believe the day I've had. When was the last time I was home?" she asked, almost to herself.

"Hey, Mom. Yesterday, I think. Who is this?" Dalton asked, as Miley and Baylor sniffed noses.

"This is Miley. She was found as a stray today. Well, her owners dumped her on the beach and Sammi brought her to me. She's going to stay with us until we find her a home. I think I have someone in mind for her though. My friend, Irina, remember her? Well, she's a huge German shepherd lover and always said to reach out to her if we get any in at the shelter. She rescued Roscoe from Ocean Pals a few years back. So, fingers crossed," Willa said, not realizing she was babbling. It had been a long, few days.

"That's cool," Dalton said. "Well, if you go inside, just be warned. Dede and Zak were making out in the living room when I came out to make some dinner and that's why we're out here. I don't need to see my sister wrapped around some guy on the couch."

"What?" Willa said, exasperated. "Okay, I'll handle it. Can Miley hang out here with you? I need to go pick up another dog and run over to see your dad. Did you ever eat?"

"No," he said over his shoulder, "And yeah, Miley can hang with us. She seems pretty chill like my man, Baylor."

Willa opened the door and saw two young adults scatter apart on the couch.

"Hey, love birds. Try and keep it rated PG-13 or less, please. Your brother wasn't happy that he saw you two making out on the couch," she called into the living room. "Dede, can you come here, please?"

Her daughter pulled away from the couch and Willa could hear her footsteps as she came through to the kitchen, "What's up, Mom?"

Willa lowered her voice, "What are you doing?"

Dede's eyebrows lifted up and pulled together as she asked, confused, "What do you mean? We're just hanging out."

"No, I mean," she squeezed her eyes shut and searched for the right words. "I mean, you're still taking your pill every day, right?"

"Mommm," Dede moaned, her face turning red in response. "We're not out here doing it on the couch or anything. We were just kissing."

"Well, okay, but if you are . . . doing it somewhere . . . you're taking the pill?"

"Jesus, yes, Mom. I'm not stupid and I don't want to be having this conversation right now with him in the other room."

"Okay, okay. Just remember to pull yourself apart long enough to let your brother back in the house and don't forget to eat. I'm going to bring home dinner from Waves. Do you want anything?"

Dede looked at her like she'd gone insane, "From Dad's restaurant?"

"Yeah, I need to talk to him about something. Do you and Zak want anything?"

"Uh, yeah, let me ask him and I want the Beyond Burger with well-done fries."

Willa pulled her daughter in for a hug, "Okay. I love you."

"I love you too, Mom," Dede said into her shoulder as she hugged her back, "Now, stop being weird and go get us some food."

Dede ran out of the room laughing as Willa jokingly tried to kick her in the butt. She missed having her kids at home and moments like this made her remember why.

"Dede, text me what Zak wants, I have to get going," Willa yelled as she walked out the door. "Same to you, Dalton," she said as she passed her son on the deck.

"Will do, Mom," he said as she hopped in her car and drove off again.

Willa pulled up to Emily's house a few minutes later and opened the door using the key she gave her before she was taken into custody. Vito ran and jumped on her, his excitement evident. His need to relieve himself was also clear as he moved from jumping on her, to jumping at the back door to the fenced yard. Willa let him out and he flew out the door and was peeing in two seconds flat.

Willa turned her attention to the smells coming from inside the house. Even though he held some of it in, Vito wasn't able to hold all his "potty" needs in over the last two days. Willa quickly cleaned up the smelly poo piles and dried pee spots he had left in a small, tiled office.

At least he kept his business to one easily cleanable area of the house, she thought to herself. Once that was taken care of, she packed him and his stuff in the car and set off to Waves.

Due to the late hour, Thomas's beachfront restaurant wasn't terribly busy when she got there. Willa left Vito in the car and went inside to look for Thomas. She greeted long-term bartender Wes and asked him to let Thomas know she was there. Thankfully, the amazing Wes poured her a glass of wine first and then went off to find Thomas in the back. When he returned, he had a funny look on his face and mouthed, "Sorry" to her as he approached.

A woman followed behind him and she came right over to Willa, reached out her hand, and introduced herself.

"Hi, I'm Ashley. I'm Thomas's girlfriend. What can I help you with?"

Doing her best to hide her surprise, Willa reached out and gave Ashley's small hand a firm shake, "I'm Willa. I just want to talk to Thomas about a personal matter."

"Well, he's busy, maybe you could—"

She was cut off when Thomas came rushing out from the kitchen towards them. He looked flustered and Willa could see Wes was peeking around the corner of the bar, slyly trying to watch the whole awkward situation unfold.

"Hey, Willa, Wes said you were here. How are you doing?" he stepped up next to Ashley and put his arm around her. "I see you met Ashley, my girlfriend."

The words came out a little jerky, like he was unsure he should call her that, but Willa ignored it. She could care less . . . although Ashley did look a lot younger than them. But that was what Thomas liked—young, blonde, and perky.

"Yep. So, look, I know this is weird, me just showing up, but I have a predicament and thought maybe you could help," Willa explained.

Thomas nodded and let her continue while Ashley stood there, eyeing her.

"I know you've always loved dogs, particularly boxers and rottweilers, so that's why I thought of you as a temporary foster for Vito—"

"Foster?" Ashley interrupted.

"Foster dog. Willa helps out at the local animal rescue. Dalton has been talking a lot about it lately. He wants to get into it too." Thomas explained.

"We have an urgent situation where we need someone to foster Vito for about a week. His current foster is . . . unavailable and will be for some time, so until the construction is done at the shelter, he needs a place to stay. He's a rottie boxer mix," Willa said.

"Okay."

"Okay, like . . . You'll think about it or okay, you'll do it?"

"I'll . . ." he caught himself, "We'll do it."

"Does he get along with other dogs?" Ashley asked. "I have a golden retriever mix."

Thomas interrupted, "If he doesn't, I'll just stay at the apartment above the restaurant while he's with us."

Willa looked back and forth between them before she put two and two together, "Oh, you two live together?"

"Yeah, she moved in three weeks ago," Thomas said as he shifted his weight from foot to foot before he changed the subject. "When do I need to come get him?"

Willa smiled, "No need. He's in the car. I'll go get him. Meet me out back."

She moved off her stool and went to get Vito before Thomas or Ashley could say anything more.

She leashed the black and tan boy up and led him to the back of the restaurant, which was also the beach.

As soon as his paws touched the soft sand, Vito's long, lean legs launched him into a frantic, goofy zoomie session. He ran from side to side, past Willa, using every inch of his leash space and spun in circles as he kicked sand up in the air. Thomas watched him with a huge smile and Ashley laughed along with him at Vito's wild antics. Willa let the three-year old boy blow off some steam since he had been cooped up for so long before she encouraged him to follow her over to the awaiting couple.

"He's so cool," Thomas said as he bent down and greeted the vivacious Vito. "What's his story?"

"He was a bait dog and was learning to trust and love people again in his foster home. He's made a complete 180 from the terrified almost painfully shy dog that came in six months ago. He might have a lot of energy tonight, because he was left alone for two days."

Thomas and Ashley looked up at her with curious eyes but didn't push the issue. Instead, Thomas asked Vito if he wanted to see the water and they walked down to the crashing waves side by side.

Willa turned to Ashley and figured she might as well be civil, "So, what brought you down to Ocean Park?"

"Umm, Thomas," she said cautiously. "We've been together for almost a year, but I was living in Wilmington, so I moved down here to be with him."

Willa nodded and wondered to herself if the kids knew about their dad's new-live-in-girlfriend. She watched Vito jump in and out of the waves before Ashley continued, "And I'm an event planner. I just joined forces with another business owner in the area. A club in downtown Ocean Park called Spinners."

Willa's head whipped around so fast she was afraid she'd be nursing a sore neck tomorrow.

Ashley looked at her expression and with a shrug asked, "Do you know it?"

Unable to hide her shock, she just nodded and said, "Yeah, one of my best friends owns it."

Chapter 18
CALEB, SEELY and Camille

As she watched Damien run around their small backyard with Seely and Duke, Camille felt her tension fade away and her lips curled into a smile as joy radiated through her body. Then, her stupid phone rang and pulled her from her happy place.

"Ugh," she groaned as she turned it over from its position on the patio table to see who was calling. The ID showed it was Willa and she hurriedly picked it up. Things at the shelter had been wild since the break-in and there was always news and exciting updates.

"Hello?"

"Camille. It's Willa. I have something I'd like to talk to you about—Could you meet me at the shelter today? Or I could come to you if that's easier?"

"Uh, sure. But what's going on? Is everything okay?"

"Yeah, everything is fine but it's just time sensitive."

"Sure, I'm free all day. Damien is just playing with the dogs right now and—"

Willa cut her off, "Oh, I wanted to tell you, Caleb is healing nicely and his one vet nurse wants to adopt him. I thought Damien might like that."

"Oh, that's wonderful. Hold on, let me tell him," she pulled the phone away from her face and called out to her son. "Damien, come here, I have some great news."

He ran over to her, which meant the two dogs, Duke and Seely ran over to her too. It was quite the audience.

"What is it?" he asked.

"Caleb is getting adopted!" she exclaimed.

Damien just looked at her, not showing a single ounce of excitement like she had been expecting.

"By who?" he asked. His face was tight and chin lifted towards the sky.

"A nurse at the vet hospital who is taking care of him. Sweetie, this is good news. I thought you'd be excited for him."

"Who told you this?" he asked, his forehead furrowed together.

Camille held up the phone, "Willa. She called and—"

Damien grabbed the phone from her and held it to his ear, while Camille stared at him, stunned and frozen in place.

"Hi, Ms. Willa," Damien said into the phone, "This is Damien. Can I see Caleb? My mom was supposed to ask if I could, but she kept telling me I had to wait until he got out of the hospital. But now you say he's getting adopted and I want to see him before he goes home and is gone forever. Please." His voice cracked as he pleaded with an equally shocked Willa.

"Well, uh, I don't see why not," Willa said, sort of taken aback by the young man's request.

"Thank you. When do you think I could see him?" asked the impatient pre-teen.

"Could you put your mom back on? I need to talk to her about this and she and I will figure out a time that works—Is that okay?"

"I guess," his voice sounded dejected, "Here she is."

He handed the phone back to his mom with a disappointed look in his eyes and his lips pulled to one side. Still trying to catch up to the situation that was going down in front of her, Camille slowly lifted the phone to her ear and said, "Hello?"

"How about you two meet me at the vet in an hour? Damien can visit with Caleb and you and I can talk. Sound good?" Willa asked directly.

"Yeah, that works," Camille babbled into the phone.

"I'll text you the address. See you soon," Willa said and hung up.

"What in the hell?" Camille said to herself as she held her quiet phone. "What just happened?"

She looked around and saw Damien was sitting in the middle of the yard with Seely and Duke, where he was petting their bellies. The dogs were loving life, but Damien looked sullen.

Camille was still trying to figure out what had just happened on that call and was wondering how Willa could bounce back from every strange situation without being thrown off beat. She shook her head to restart her brain and called out to Damien once she got her bearings back.

"Damien. You got your wish. We're going to visit Caleb in an hour."

Her son jumped up from his spot in the grass, interrupting the meditation session of the two dogs that sat next to him and yelled, "Are you serious?"

"Yup," she smiled at him as he jumped up and down in celebration. Duke and Seely joined him and barked and bounced around him, even though they had no idea why they were so excited and happy.

Dogs—the best friends and hype men you could ever have.

Camille pulled open the door to the vet's office and looked around the reception area for Willa. She spotted her talking to a female vet, who looked familiar, and walked over to them, Damien hot on her heels.

"Hey, how's Caleb doing?" Camille asked Willa.

"Hey. He's doing much better. This is Dr. Izzy. She's been taking care of Caleb since the break-in," Willa said.

"Oh yeah, I remember you," Camille said as she reached out her hand to greet Dr. Izzy, "You were the one who yelled at that police officer and then came in to help Caleb. Thanks for letting us see him. I'm Camille and this is my son, Damien."

"Yeah, Hi, I remember you too. You were a big help that day," she said to Camille before she turned her attention to Damien. "And I hear you were a big help to Caleb too. You found him when he was a stray, right? And you made your mom take him to Ocean Pals?"

Damien nodded before answering, "Yeah, but I hate that he got hurt in the attack. He was there because of me." His eyes and head dropped to stare at the floor as his voice cracked a bit.

Dr. Izzy shook her head and said, "Oh Damien, you're the reason he's finding his forever home now. You put him in the position to find his people and you should be so proud of that. Willa told me you'd like to see him."

His eyes lifted to hers and a small smile pulled at his lips, "Yes, please." And then he added, "And I'd like to meet the person adopting him too."

Dr. Izzy nodded and led them all back to a small room past the reception area. The name on the door suggested that this was Dr. Izzy's personal office and when she opened the door and let them in, an excited Caleb greeted them.

"Caleb," Damien yelled, his elation evident.

He ran towards the dog and dropped to his knees to greet him. Caleb kissed the young man who saved him anywhere he could, from his knees to his hair. Damien laughed, scratched the dog's ears, and enveloped him in long-held hugs and kisses.

A young vet nurse with dark hair and kind eyes held the leash connected to Caleb's collar. She smiled and laughed along with Damien as she watched the two boys interact. She pulled herself up from the floor where she was seated and held her hand out to Camille.

"Hi, I'm Sasha. I'm the one who put in an adoption application on Caleb."

"Hey, nice to meet you and thanks for meeting with us. Caleb means a lot to Damien and he's been very invested in him finding a good home. We really appreciate you taking care of him. He's a sweet boy."

Damien looked up at Sasha as Caleb kissed his cheek over and over again, obviously remembering him from when he rescued him at the park.

"Are you going to take good care of him?" Damien asked, his voice strong and deep. So deep that it took Camille by surprise. Man, her boy was growing up right before her eyes.

"Yeah, I'm going to take great care of him, if they approve the adoption. I'm still waiting to hear back, but he'll live with me and will have a big backyard to play in and he'll be able to relax on the couch and sleep in my bed if he wants. I already bought a bunch of treats and have a nice bed for him to sleep on if he wants some space. My old dog passed away a few months ago and I wasn't ready to adopt another dog until Caleb came around. He's been helping mend my broken heart," she said to Damien. She talked to him like he was her peer, but he didn't say anything in response.

"Hun, it sounds like he's going to be really spoiled and living the good life," Camille said, as she tried to encourage him to accept that his friend was going to a loving home.

"What about walks? You probably work a lot," Damien said as he held his hands out in a motion that gestured towards the vet office. "Will you take him out on walks every day? I don't think he should go home with you if he won't get the right amount of exercise."

"Damien—" Camille threatened but Sasha cut her off.

"No, it's okay. He's concerned about his well-being and I can appreciate that," she said. "What if you helped me walk him?"

Damien just gave her a confused look, so Sasha turned towards Camille and then looked back to Damien before she continued, "Willa told me we live in the same neighborhood. I'd love to hire you to help walk Caleb while I'm at work on the weekends or in the evening after school. If it's okay with your mom."

Damien looked from Sasha to Camille and back again, before he stood up, put his hands on his mom's shoulders, and asked, "Mom? Can I?"

His voice carried so much emotion and hope that Camille couldn't help but nod her head in agreement. Damien's eyes grew to the size of saucers before he turned and in an unexpected move, hugged Camille and then Sasha before he returned to Caleb to hug him and explain their new situation. His laughter and excitement filled the room with love.

Camille turned to Sasha and through her huge grin said, "Thank you so much. You don't have to do that, but he would really love to walk him sometimes. And you don't have to pay him."

Sasha waved her off, "Of course I do. A young man like him, who loves dogs, could really start his own dog walking business and make some good money. There's a big need for reliable walkers in Ocean Park. Not too many that would get in the way of his schoolwork or anything but enough to keep him busy on the weekends and holidays, if that's something he'd want to do. I heard about him saving Caleb and how he's so attached to him and Willa said he'd be a great dog walker, so I figured why not? Plus, he'd be really helping me out on the days that I work late or weekends when I work overtime."

Camille just smiled and thanked the woman again, amazed at how the situation was unfolding before her. Talk about fate.

"So, Damien, do you think Sasha should be able to adopt Caleb?" Willa asked. "You're the last deciding vote. If you say yes, then he gets to go home with her. We already checked everything out and we think she'll be a great mom to Caleb."

Damien looked at Caleb and whispered something in his ear. The dog lifted his nose and placed a wet kiss on his cheek. "Yeah, I think so too," he said with a smile.

Camille and Willa excused themselves from the vet's office and let Caleb, Damien, and Sasha hang out for a few minutes while they talked.

"So, I wanted to ask you about helping more at the shelter." Willa just dove right in.

"Oh, sure. What do you have in mind?"

"The board asked me to be the new director—"

"Oh my god, that's wonderful. Congratulations!" Camille said with a big smile.

"Thank you, but I told them I'd only do it if you were my co-director."

Camille looked at Willa like she had three heads, "Huh?"

"I don't want to take on a full-time role with Dalton still in the beginning of his mental health diagnosis and I like being mostly retired and available for my family and friends as needed. I know you wanted to take on more at the shelter and your legal experience would be a wonderful asset. Plus, we work well together and it'll be mostly part-time so you can still work on your own law stuff. I just think together we can really make a difference and get the shelter back on track. What'd you say?"

Camille felt her face pull into a big smile as she said, "Yeah, let's do it!"

Chapter 19

SAILOR and JC

The front door slammed shut and JC called out to Ryan, "I'm in here, babe!"

He could hear Ryan greet Sailor before his footsteps signaled that he was coming down the short hallway towards their eat-in kitchen. When he rounded the corner, his facial expression was a mixture of surprise with a large chunk still showing that was pissed off about their adoption fight the other night.

"What's all this?" he asked, his voice cold.

"I made us dinner," JC explained, "I know you're the amazing chef, but I figured you deserved a night off from cooking, so I stepped in and am doing my best. Here, have a glass of wine."

He pushed a freshly poured glass of pinot noir towards Ryan and watched as he took a sip. Ryan's gaze never left JC's as he eyed him warily.

"What's really going on?" Ryan asked.

JC continued to chop mushrooms for their salad and gave his husband a little shrug. "I know you're pissed at me, for a lot of things, but I have some news."

Ryan started to chop up an onion but stayed quiet to let JC talk.

"After some soul searching and some business developments, I . . . I want to say that I'm ready to start the adoption classes whenever you want. I know this is important to us and we need to move forward on it if we're really going to do it. I don't want to keep saying, "Yeah, we'll get to it when . . ." or "Maybe next year or the next."

Ryan gave him a look as he threw the chopped onions into the salad and asked, "What changed your mind? And what business developments?"

"I found a business partner the day after our fight but didn't want to say anything until we made it official. A woman named Ashley, who is an expert at planning events and who just moved here to be with her boyfriend. She seems to have a good business sense and her ideas for the club are amazing. It could really transform Spinners into something super successful and make us a hot spot here in Ocean Park. But after talking with her, I realized that I don't need to work night and day at the club if she signs on. I started thinking about us and our life and how we want to grow our family together. With things looking up at the club, I feel a huge burden has been lifted from my shoulders. I'm ready to talk about adoption and take the classes. Don't get me wrong, I'm totally and completely terrified—but I'm also ready to make that leap with you by my side—if you still want me."

Ryan pulled in a long breath before he smiled at his nervous husband, "I absolutely still want to be with you. And I'm proud of you for finding a business partner. I really hope you two can turn the club around together. I'm hesitant to get excited about your change of heart on the foster and adoption front, so I'll believe it when I see it, but I'm glad you're open to exploring it with me."

Ryan stepped towards JC and pulled him into a long hug. The two men relaxed into each other's arms and held their embrace for a good 30-seconds before they pulled away enough to end their fight with an equally long kiss. Ryan finally pulled back to let JC focus on his dinner prep, but not before he gave his round butt a slap.

"That's for being an ass and staying out all night. You had Sailor and I worried," he said with a laugh.

"Speaking of Sailor," JC said with a smile of his own, "I got a text today that there's a family interested in meeting her. She might be finding her forever home."

"Aww," Ryan said as he bent down to pet the pretty girl. "That's wonderful, but I'll really miss her."

Sailor leaned into Ryan's hand and looked up at him before she jumped up and offered him a kiss on his lips.

"I think she'll miss us too, but the people interested in her are big into mountain biking, hiking, and running and they want her to join them in their adventures. She'd love that stuff. I'm meeting them tomorrow evening at 6 p.m., if you'd like to join. Willa is overseeing the adoption, so she'll be there too."

"Sounds good. I'll try to be there if I can get away for a little bit. We've been swamped lately, even without the tourists around. Maybe it's the holiday crowd, but I could really use a break," he said as he curled up on the floor with Sailor.

"Me and you both, babe!" JC chimed in from the kitchen. "Plan us a vacation! We need it before life gets more hectic when we have kids in the house."

Ryan winked at him and pulled out his phone.

"Where did you have in mind?"

"Anywhere, as long as it's with you," JC said before he blew a kiss to Ryan and turned to pull the pasta dish out of the oven.

Ryan unlocked his phone and started searching in a vacation app for rentals within a four-hour drive. He browsed for a while—saving a few homes that looked promising and that were dog friendly. He knew Sailor was meeting with a potential adoptive family tomorrow, but he loved having a dog in the house again and even though he hadn't told JC yet, he decided that he'd like them to keep fostering.

His phone dinged, signaling that he had a new text message, and he heard JC's phone do the same from its place on their kitchen island. JC was spooning pasta with marinara sauce onto two plates and his oven mitts seemed to be making the process a million times harder, so Ryan asked if he'd like some help.

"No, I'm good, but can you check my phone?" he asked, his voice strained as he concentrated on the task that always looked so easy when Ryan did it.

"Sure," Ryan said as he opened the text he got while he stood up to look at JC's phone too.

"They're both from Camille. I think she sent us the same thing. It's a link to something."

He clicked on her message then walked over to stand next to JC when he saw it was a video of a live online news conference.

The video started out with a red headline that flew across the screen, screaming for the viewer's attention. Loud, dramatic music played in step with intense graphics before a pretty, middle-aged newscaster came on the screen with a serious look on her face.

"We have breaking news out of Ocean Pines and Berlin tonight," she said in her methodical newscaster voice. "A man's body has been found off Route 589. Investigators are on the scene and we're going there for their statement to the public."

JC and Ryan looked at each other in confusion, not understanding why Camille would send them this news video.

"A local man is dead after being shot in the head. Police are still searching for the shooter but have video surveillance of the crime," another newscaster said—as they stood live in front of Ocean Downs Casino.

"We're here, live, with detectives from the Ocean Park Police Department. Do you think this is an act of random violence? Should the public be worried?"

The camera panned back to reveal a tall detective who shook his head at the question.

"No, we have reason to believe Mr. Randle was involved in local crime and suspect that he ran into some trouble with his associates. We believe this was a sanctioned hit and do not want the public to be fearful that a random murderer is on the loose. We have a few leads on who the perpetrators are and why they committed this crime."

"Mr. Randle?" JC said in shock.

"Who's that?" Ryan asked, with furrowed brows, not making the connection to the only Mr. Randle in their lives.

"Can you walk us through the surveillance video we're about to play?"

"Sure, but please be aware of its graphic content that's not suitable for minors."

The video moved from an image of the detective to one of black and white security camera footage that looked down over the side of the casino building and parking lot.

"Here the victim is seen walking out of the casino and appears to be texting on his phone. His head is down and he doesn't seem to notice the white van that's circling around behind him. He puts his phone into his pocket as the van gets closer and this is where we see a man walk out from behind the first row of parked cars. The victim seems to recognize the man and walks towards him. When the van pulls up behind the two men, who look to be in a heated conversation, the man on the right pulls out a gun and, well, you can see for yourself that he takes one shot and kills the victim. He and another man move the body into the van and that's the last image we have of them. If you or anyone you know recognize the men or the vehicle, please contact the police."

"How did you come across this information?" the newscaster asked.

"No one reported anything at the casino that night, so we didn't know about the shooting until a woman walking her dog came across the body this morning. We identified the body as Steve Randle and found that he was a person of interest in another case we're investigating and that he was labeled as missing. We knew his last known location was the casino off Racetrack Road, so we got a warrant for their security footage and here we are. Now, we're looking for information on the shooters."

"Can you elaborate on the investigation into Mr. Randle?"

"Typically, we do not comment on on-going cases, but the victims of Mr. Randle's crimes have asked that we're open about the situation as the public might be able to assist them going forward," he cleared his throat and continued.

"Mr. Steve Randle was the director at the local animal rescue, Ocean Pals. Recently, there was a break-in at their facility, which left thousands of dollars in damage and injured two dogs. Mr. Randle was the last person known to be at the shelter before the break-in and we later found out that he was there and was beaten up in the process. Then, he went to the casino with an accomplice, where he spent the next 46 hours gambling at the poker and craps tables. His accomplice left before him. She is now in custody and has been cooperating with the investigation and provided us with most of our inside information. What we know is that Mr. Randle was embezzling from the shelter to cover his gambling debts. The break-in was done to target him for not paying back those debts. He was at the casino trying to make back the money he owed and we believe he was killed off because he was seen as a liability."

The newscaster shook his head, "Wow, thank you, Detective. Newly appointed co-directors, Willa Atkins and Camille DiAngelo, join us now. Thank you for being here, ladies. What do you want the public to know about these crimes?"

"We'd like the public to know that immediate action was taken to appoint us as the new co-directors of the shelter and that systems are already being put into action that will never allow a financial crime like this to happen again at Ocean Pals. We found temporary foster homes for all the animals displaced by the break-in and are a few days away from being able to welcome them all back to the shelter and to re-open to the public. There was a lot of damage done to the shelter from the break-in and while that is almost all completed, the emotional damage is still being repaired," Willa said to the newscaster. Her words came out choppy and jittery, which showed that she was nervous, but her shoulders stayed tall and she put on a brave face for the camera.

Camille jumped in and her words flowed eloquently, like she'd been speaking in front of a camera forever, "We'd also like to thank the public for their outpouring of help and support during this difficult time. We had many new volunteers show up when we put out the word that we needed help and we can't thank you all enough. We wouldn't have been able to do this on our own. We hope to recover all the money stolen by Steve Randle by the end of next year. We will not let him, nor the criminals that broke into our facility and injured our dogs, stop us from helping the needy animals of

Ocean Park. We strive to be the best advocates for animals in the area and we promise to continue helping those in need for many years to come."

The newscaster nodded and with concern in his voice asked, "And how are the dogs who were injured? Are they healing or available for adoption yet?"

Willa spoke more confidently this time, "Both dogs are healing nicely. We'd like to thank Dr. Izzy and Dr. Dylan for their continued effort and treatment of our animals. They came to our rescue after the break-in and took wonderful care of Hollywood and Caleb."

She smiled and turned to Camille, who took over, "Hollywood is available for adoption. He's a 155-pound great dane, so if you're interested in learning more about him, please contact the shelter. We're still not open to the public yet, but someone is always there to answer phones during business hours. Caleb is still recovering but we're happy to say that his adoption went through last night and he'll be going to a wonderful home once he's released from the vet hospital. We have a lot of other fantastic dogs and cats who are looking for their forever families, so please check our website and social media sites to see their pictures and bios. We're hoping to open soon, so stop by to meet them in person once we're back up and running again."

JC turned to Ryan as the newscaster thanked the interviewees and the video screen went blank.

"Holy shit!" he said as he ran his hands over his forehead. "Steve is dead and he stole from the freakin' shelter. What the hell?"

Ryan shook his head, "Willa and Camille didn't say anything to you about this?"

"No," he said as his phone rang. "It's Willa."

He swiped up to answer and said into the phone, "Ladies, you have a lot of explaining to do!"

Laughter came from the other end, "We're both here on speaker phone," Willa said. "We're sorry you had to find out this way, but the board wanted us to announce it on the news first after we were told about Steve's death."

"Did they find his killers?" JC asked.

"No, but they have a pretty good idea who did it. Emily uncovered all the pertinent details and the police are out looking for the men in question. They think it was his bookie and his crew. They're the ones who broke into the shelter," Willa said.

They talked a little more about the newscast and Steve's embezzlement before Willa and Camille filled JC in on the other terrible things Steve did at the shelter.

After he let the information sink in that some of his favorite animals were killed instead of adopted, JC asked the question they all were thinking, "So, am I the only one who is glad the bastard is dead?"

Chapter 20

JC, WILLA, CAMILLE and SAMMI

At 6 p.m. the next day, JC, Ryan, Willa, and Sailor waited at the park across the street from Ocean Pals for Sailor's meet-and-greet with her potential adoptive parents.

"I need to get back to work soon, so if this goes longer than 30 minutes, I'll need to head out," Ryan said to the group as they watched the street. He leaned down to talk to Sailor, "Sweetie, if you do get to go home with these people, just remember your manners and know that we love you very much. We'll miss you but will be so happy that you finally found your forever home. Don't forget about us though."

He placed a few kisses on the top of her head and she jumped to cover his face and ears in her signature nibbley kisses.

"Here they are," said Willa as a red Jeep Wrangler pulled up to the curb and a young couple hopped out and headed over to them. They couldn't take their eyes off Sailor as they walked up and they both dropped to the ground to meet her on her level when they got to the group.

"Hi, pretty girl!" the woman said as she scratched and pet an excited Sailor. "Aren't you so nice and beautiful?"

Sailor moved between the two and jumped up and down on them, forgetting all about the manners Ryan had just mentioned to her.

"Hi girl, I'm Brett and this is Kieara. We're so excited to meet you," the man said as Sailor bounced up onto his lap.

They finally looked up to the people in the group and introductions were made. Willa let Ryan and JC speak about Sailor's behavior in their house and they ranted and raved about the brindle girl, but didn't sugar coat her less-than-stellar traits either.

"She does jump up a lot and can get nibbley with her kisses, so we tried working with her on staying calm to greet people and to keep kisses to a minimum when she's super excited. That's typically when she gets nippy. It's almost like she's so jacked up to meet people that she gives aggressive kisses," JC explained. "She's smart though and picked up on the commands we gave her without a problem. She just needs more time with them. We've only had her for about a week."

The couple asked a few questions and talked about how they planned to take her on all their adventures. She'd have free reign of the house, if she wanted while they were out, but they also mentioned that Kieara worked from home, so Sailor wouldn't be alone a lot.

"She loves her people, so that'll be good for her," Ryan said before he glanced at his watch again. "I have to get back to work, but it was nice meeting you."

He leaned down to pet Sailor one more time and whispered a few things in her ear. She looked up at him like she understood and gave him one last kiss on the lips before she went over and sat down between Brett and Kieara.

Ryan laughed, "I think she likes you guys."

Then he and JC shared a quick kiss before he jogged over to his car and left for work.

"If you want to walk her around the park a little, feel free. She does need some work on her leash manners, so just keep the leash looped around your wrist nice and tight," Willa said to the adventurous couple.

They took off with a prancing Sailor, who pulled hard on the leash.

"I hope she doesn't blow it. She pulls like she's a 50-pound dog, not a 25-pounder," JC said to Willa.

"Hopefully not. They look like they're in love with her already. Hey, how are things going at the club? I hear you have a new partner?" Willa said.

"They're good, but how'd you know? I haven't told anyone about the partnership except Ryan."

"Ashley told me."

"What now?"

"Yeah, I met her when I took Vito over to Thomas's restaurant. They're fostering him," Willa said, waiting to see if JC could put the pieces together.

"What do you mean? They're going to foster him? She knows Thomas, your ex?"

"Yup, they live together."

JC's brow pulled together, his mouth hung open a little, and his head tilted to the side. He stared at her for a few more seconds before it dawned on him. With a gasp, he said, "Wait a second! Thomas is Ashley's business owning boyfriend?"

"Yup."

"Holy crap, Willa, I had no idea."

"JC, it's no big deal. It just took me by surprise."

"But he's, like, over 20 years older than her."

"Oh no, that makes her just his type. Hopefully, she's good for him," Willa said with a shrug.

"Damn, you're being awfully cool about this."

"I don't really care what he does, as long as it doesn't hurt our kids. We weren't right for each other and I sure as hell don't want to be with him, so it's really no sweat off my back."

JC was quiet for a few beats before he asked, "Do you ever think of dating again?"

"Nah," Willa said with a shake of her head. "I mean, if it happens, it happens, but I'm perfectly content on my own right now."

They were pulled from their conversation as Sailor came running over to them dragging a laughing Brett behind her.

"We'll take her!" he said through gulps of air. "She's just what we wanted in a dog. A smart, sweet active pup who will join us on all our adventures and trips. What else do we need to do to make it official?"

Kieara ran up behind them, holding a heavy poop bag, "She's wild, but man, she's awesome."

Willa clapped her hands together, "We're so glad you like her. You're good to go. I already called your vet and checked in with your references. This meet-and-greet was just to make sure you all clicked and wanted to move forward. I have some stuff for you in the car, plus a bag of food to get you started. It's what she ate in the shelter and in foster care, but if you want to switch her to a different brand, just slowly introduce it with her old food. So instead of giving her a ¾ cup of her old kibble, do ½ cup of the old with ¼ of the new food for a few days and slowly decrease the old for the new until you're out of the old food. This will help her acclimate to the new food without having any digestive issues, like runny poop, upset stomach, or vomiting."

JC said his goodbyes to Sailor and waited for Willa at his car while she finished up with Sailor's new pawrents. Once in their Jeep, Sailor plopped herself proudly on Kieara's lap and her wide grin said it all. She was happier than could be and she knew she had hit the jackpot and found her forever home.

Willa walked back to JC and put her arm over his shoulder as he watched his foster dog ride off into the sunset to her new life.

"How're you doing?" she asked.

"It's a lot harder than I thought it'd be. We only had her with us for a week and I wanted her to find her forever home, but I feel like she took a little bit of my heart with her. I'm excited for her, but sad for me, you know, even though I know it's silly because she looked so happy."

"That's how fostering works. You get attached and then they leave. You know it's going to happen and you can try and prepare for it, but you still feel sad when they're gone," Willa said. "But just wait until you get a picture of her on her first hike or they send you a text saying they love her to pieces and can't imagine life without her. Then you'll know why we do it and why we put ourselves through that initial pain ... because those texts, pictures, and updates make it all worth it. Just wait and see."

"But they don't have my number or anything ..."

"Yeah, they do. I gave it to them and told them to keep in touch. They said they would and asked for your last name to add you on social media. I have so many Facebook friends that are adopters of my former foster dogs. You can keep tabs on them and you get to see the wonderful lives they end up living after their time at the shelter."

JC pulled Willa into his body and wrapped his arms around her, "Thank you. You're amazing. I love you, dear friend."

"I love you too. Now, let's go get a drink!"

JC and Willa pulled up to The Salty Crab and each found a parking space. With the holidays right around the corner, Ocean Park had a few more tourists than it normally did during the off-season. Summer was packed, fall was busy, winter was like a ghost town, and spring started the cycle all over again as people started to sprinkle into town.

"I texted Camille and Sammi too. They'll be here in a few," JC said as he and Willa found a table in the enclosed porch on the dock that backed up to the bay. Propane gas heaters filled the space with warm air and made it bearable to sit out by the rippling water. Boats bobbed up and down at the nearby marina and seagulls lined the docks like a picturesque postcard.

After a few minutes, Camille and Sammi joined them and everyone ordered their drinks and some appetizers. French fries and a gin and tonic for Sammi, onion rings and a glass of white wine for Camille, fried mushrooms and a red wine for Willa, and cheese fries and a beer for JC.

While they waited for their food, they sipped on their drinks and caught up on the last few days.

"How was your date with Trevor?" Willa asked Sammi.

"It was good. He has some financial baggage, which freaked me out at first, but after thinking about it, at our age, who doesn't have some serious baggage? You all know I do," she said with a chuckle. "But we're going out again tomorrow and I think I might . . . really like him."

The table erupted in laughter, squeals and whistles as Sammi burrowed her head into her hands. When she finally pulled her hands away, her face was red, but a big smile was set across her face.

"You guys are just what I needed. Thank you for being here for me . . . and for embarrassing the hell out of me from time to time too," she said with another laugh.

Camille jumped in, "Yeah, I'm so glad we all met at the shelter this year. I feel like I've known you all forever, but it's only been a few months. I'm really looking forward to working with you at the shelter and making some real change for the animals here in Ocean Park."

"Me too. I keep forgetting that Camille and Sammi are new to our little group. Willa, you finally have some other people to boss around besides me," JC joked to her with a jab of his elbow.

"Oh, come on," she said back to him, her voice dry. "You know you love it."

She stuck her tongue out at him and then gave him a warm smile.

"In all seriousness though, now that the shelter is almost back to normal and Camille and I will be running the ship, I'm more thankful than ever for all your friendships and hard work at Ocean Pals. This is a team effort and I'd say we make a pretty damn good team."

A waiter arrived with their food and interrupted their group gab session. The smell of the fried food wafted up from the table and mixed with the warm, propane-fueled air.

"This is my cheat meal, ladies," JC said as he held his foamy beer toward the center of the table, while he waited for everyone to join him.

They all brought their drinks together and clinked.

"We've had a wild few weeks. Here's hoping next year brings a lot less drama and a lot more fun," JC said.

"Here, here!" Willa and Sammi said in unison.

They all laughed and took long sips of their drinks before Camille added, "Yeah, after all the drama this year, what else could go wrong?"

JC groaned, Willa covered her face with her hands, and Sammi stared at her with wide eyes.

"Camille, don't jinx it!" JC cried.

"What?" she said, as she held her hands out in front of her in the universal "What did I say wrong" stance. "Seriously, after everything we went through. What else could top that?"

The group groaned again as the waiter brought another round of drinks to the table.

"Keep 'em coming," Willa said to the man before she let the group in on a little secret. "You're all involved in the animal rescue world now. You gotta know that things are always dramatic, never easy, always dirty, and totally, 100% worth it. Get ready for a wild ride—there will always be animals that need us."

She held her glass up high for another cheers, "To Ocean Pals!"

The other three joined in and yelled loudly over the bay, "To Ocean Pals!"

Acknowledgments

Thank you to all my friends and family who supported me in this endeavor, who read the many first drafts, and who let me talk their ear off as I worked through this process of fear, doubt, excitement, and a tornado of other chaotic emotions.

To my first reader – **Mom** – Thank you for everything. You're my best friend and rock in life. You didn't laugh at me when I said I wrote a book and pushed me to continue when I doubted myself.

To my wonderful husband – **Corey** – Thank you for your endless support and belief in me. You pick me up when I'm down and are the reason I wrote this book in the first place. I'm the luckiest woman in the world to be able to call you my partner in life and I couldn't have done any of this without you by my side.

To my beta readers – **Marie, Lea, Mom, Michelle, Elaine and Adriane** – I'll say it again, even though I feel like I can't say it enough, thank you thank you thank you for reading, editing, and consulting on this book! I felt like a fish out of water most of the time during this editing and publishing journey and your help, guidance, and critiques helped make this book what it is today. Thank you from the bottom of my heart for your time and effort.

About the Author

Jamie Mitchell Hadzick is a first-time author, animal lover, former gymnast, and animal shelter volunteer.

When she's not writing, she can be found eating, walking her dog, Duke, snuggling with her three cats, or sipping wine with her husband.

She lives in the mountains, has lots of deer friends, and is excited to continue to explore the wild world of self-publishing.

To learn more, visit:
www.jamiemitchellhadzick.com

Instagram:
@jamie9705

Printed in Great Britain
by Amazon

85786079R00148